T0198594

Till Dope Do Us Part

MICHAEL C. PARKER

iUniverse®

TILL DOPE DO US PART

iUniverse books may be ordered through booksellers or by contacting:

iUniverse
1663 Liberty Drive
Bloomington, IN 47403
www.iuniverse.com
844-349-9409

Because of the dynamic nature of the Internet, any web addresses or links contained in this book may have changed since publication and may no longer be valid. The views expressed in this work are solely those of the author and do not necessarily reflect the views of the publisher, and the publisher hereby disclaims any responsibility for them.

Any people depicted in stock imagery provided by Getty Images are models, and such images are being used for illustrative purposes only. Certain stock imagery © Getty Images.

ISBN: 978-1-6632-4673-8 (sc)
ISBN: 978-1-6632-4674-5 (e)

Library of Congress Control Number: 2022919092

Print information available on the last page.

iUniverse rev. date: 02/23/2023

TILL DOPE DO US PART brings the underworld into the 21ˢᵗ century when an Italian mob boss who supplies the inner city takes ill and is forced to pass the family business to his only heir, Ferrell Valentino. Ferrell has played the shadow long enough and has planned for the day when she'd meet the legend behind his name, but she's green to the ways and means of her family riches. The Don protects her the best way he knows how by offering a merger with the inner city's Lion Family whom he supplies. Blood is mixed and the two worlds exchange vows with an offer the streets cannot refuse when the first Black man is inducted into the Italian mob family as a Boss of Bosses alongside its First Lady.

Dedicated to the memory of:

Richard Lee Parker and Sonya Lovelace-Jones, for we may have lost you in the flesh, but the universe birthed two stars that will shine forever. R.I.P. 2019

Dedication

WE CELEBRATE LIFE NOT BY OUR ACCOMPLISHMENTS but alongside those who give us strength, encouragement, and make personal sacrifices to see our goals fulfilled despite the obstacles. Some remained for an hour, others a few weeks or months, and a few held on throughout the years until this day. To you all, I am most humbled by your friendship, family devotion, and business tenacity.

LaTonya N. Lovelace, the woman who stood by my side in love and back-to-back against all odds. When it was said the grass is always greener on the other side, you rolled up your sleeves and planted the seeds to make ours the greenest grass on the block. The love is reciprocated and the loyalty infinite.

Asiana Coleman, for your typing and creative designs for Divine Diva on the cover, you are the embodiment of inspiration.

To Kyla McGinister, in doing your part in making this book possible, your opinions always mattered and the smallest voice in the room is often the biggest boss in the room.

To Kenny McGinister, for taking time to retype the manuscript and keeping us on the deadline with the publisher, your skill is invaluable.

Shirley Lovelace and Gloria D. Parker, your criticism was

the push we needed to get us across the finish line. Love does conquer all.

To my daughter Ahlisha (Alexis, Ayana, and Asia) and son Jamyrin Williams, we the best!!!

And last but not least, to our followers. Thank you all for your inspiration.

Chapter
1

"YES SIR, MR. VALENTINO. I'LL BE THERE."

"Lion," he chuckled between a saver cough before hanging up.

It had been a long time since I called Andrew by his surname, Valentino. He rarely called for a sit-down unless something had run afoul, or new orders were being issued by the heads of the families to the streets. Some voices do not need aggression for you to hear its authority. Although I remained the Lion of the city streets, there were by far other predators that lurked the underworld jungles, and traps man-made as well as natural viruses that were as vicious as a worldwide pandemic. His call became my third matter to attend to; the Brotherhood meeting was my first order of business.

I came up off the Lodge Freeway and made a right turn on Livernois just as my phone went off. It was Medina. It was her birthday, and although it was on a much lighter note, it was nevertheless just as important, if not my highest priority of the day. The Brotherhood Nightclub was on the corner of Fenkell and Livernois, in eye shot as I looked at her call. Answering would have only diverted my attention even further than the call I had just taken.

"What up doe, Lion?" Blast asked as he opened my door before I could put the car in park.

I didn't say anything immediately, not until I was out of the Jaguar and had looked the main street over.

"I'm late," I finally responded, heading out of the parking lot towards the nightclub.

"Not by my watch," he opined.

Once inside the club, everything quickly came to order. The heads of the families were seated and acknowledged by the plaques on their tables. I walked straight to the chairman's table positioned on the dancefloor, being flanked by four of my handpicked men.

"Good afternoon, ladies and gentlemen," I said to bring things to order, as I sat down.

"Lion," came from various corners of the club.

"Are all of the families present?" I asked.

"Everyone with the exception of," Castro, my first lieutenant, cleared his throat before saying, "the Rakehell family."

The Rakehell family had been suspended from all family meetings for 180 days and fined $50,000 dollars, to go into the families PR treasury, for the chain of deaths committed by the Highland Park and Puritan region over turf wars. I assumed it could be the possible reason Andrew was calling me for a sit-down. Needless bloodshed drew attention that made it bad for business, especially when the higher-up's caught wind of blood flowing in the gutters from the streets.

"Good," I glanced over at the only empty table in the room, then interposed, "then we can proceed."

"I called this meeting," I started, "and we're here in daylight hours because of the severity of a problem that affects everyone here. I don't want to take up much time on anything other than this issue," I said. "If there are any individual matters that can be addressed on a smaller setting, than I would be delighted to mediate, if need be, at that time. Can we all agree on this?"

The agreement was reached by the customary high raising of hats and hands.

"Wonderful," I said. "Majority carries. We'll move straight to the matter at hand. As most of you are aware of by now, the massive oil spill that has occurred off the coast has affected transport of our various investments and because the entire world has turned its attention in that direction, I have taken all deals off the table with our supplier."

One hand raised.

"Yes," I acknowledged.

"Showboat, representing the Sixty-Nine family," he introduced himself. "So does this mean we're facing a drought?" he asked.

"No, it doesn't," I replied. "For now, you're here to accept or reject me as your supplier. This shipment was supposed to be cheaper than your last supply. But with that off the table, I can only provide you with a limited supply to hold you over at the same price of your original purchase order. So, the deal I'm offering is this — you can leave your investments on the table for a future run, which I cannot guarantee it will be the same quality product, or you can cash out with me by using your present holdings."

The club was filled with mixed feelings as far as I could tell by the small whispers amongst themselves. But there was one sure sign that was expressed by the entire room, and that was no one wanted to appear as though they could not afford to take my offer.

"So this makes you our new supplier?" Showboat weighed in.

"For now, yes," I said, "if you want to call it that."

"What else would you call it?" he inquired."

Gratitude!" I snapped.

He was silenced by the hand touching his shoulder. Showboat was second-in-command of the Sixty-Nine family and was simply out to live up to his name. Casablanca, the hand that touched his shoulder, prided himself as being slow to speak and twice as flamboyant. He nodded his approval in accepting my proposal.

"If there's nothing further," I concluded, "then there's only one matter left to be voted on, that there be no increase in your sales to the streets as long as supply can meet demand. Can we all agree?"

Everyone approved, and the vote carried.

"Then I thank you all for being on time and you'll be individually contacted for distribution." The meeting was closed by my gavel, and my social time was cut short as I passed everyone just as fast as I had entered the club. My second meeting would be more celestial.

Chapter
2

3:45 P.M. BETTER TO BE SAFE THAN SORRY.

Although the meeting at the Brotherhood Club was behind me, a burgundy GTO bounced in and out of my rearview mirror as I came up off the highway and made it to West Bloomfield, an upscale community that made it easy for unusual activity to stand out like a sore thumb. The driver of the GTO was a female and may have thought she was being inconspicuous, but her passenger who had his seat reclined drew my attention by the way he kept lifting his head up every few minutes and back down out of sight once she switched lanes, so I was sure it was not the cops tailing me. The only problem was they kept at such a distance that I could not make out their license plates number without giving away my awareness. It would have been easy to attribute it to my own paranoia, so I took precautionary measures and drove a couple of miles beyond my turn and did a U-turn through the Bank of America parking lot before heading to Medina's house. I no longer saw the GTO, but I did wonder how long it had been following behind me before I noticed them. By the time my intuition kicked in that told me I should have kept driving, I had already pulled into Medina's driveway and had my fingers on the ignition key, turning the car off.

I got out of the car and walked up to the house, and looked back down the road just as Medina opened the front door.

"Why don't you ever use your key?" she asked, wearing a pink thigh-high bath robe and fuzzy slippers.

I stepped inside, closed the door behind me and looked at my watch. "I thought you'd be dressed by now."

"I am dressed, it's my birthday," she smiled.

"I know that. Happy birthday! Is that what you're wearing?"

Medina opened her robe and let it drop to the floor and stepped out of her slippers. "How's this for a birthday suit?" she asked, then turned around and stuck her ass out towards me. "Spank me for a long life to live."

I decided to play along since it was her birthday, walked closer and spanked her twice before she jumped back, laughing.

"Somebody's naughty," she said, then walked into my arms for a kiss.

"I see your gifts arrived," I could barely get the words out between kisses.

Medina snatched her tongue out of my mouth. "About those," she said, before I stuck my tongue back in her mouth and grabbed two palms full of her ass and squeezed them like cotton candy.

As things began heating up, Medina started unbuckling my pants and unbuttoning my shirt roughly.

"I thought you wanted to go out," I said, reaching down and grabbing her by her thighs and lifting her in the air as she wrapped her legs around my waist and her arms around my neck. We kept the kissing up between talking and me walking to the bedroom.

"That's because you never asked me what I wanted to do for my birthday."

"So we're cancelling dinner?" I asked as we reached her king size bed and I let her down on top of the apple green satin sheets and began taking the rest of my clothes off.

"Here's the deal honey bunny," she said, taking my shirt off and tossing it on the chair along with my underwear. "For the next several hours until my birthday ends, you're mine. I'm not about to be paraded all over town in a celebration that's supposed to be for me while you secretly broker business deals while your goon squad and strangers I don't know bring me gifts that I can't pronounce all for the sake of impressing you." She pulled me on top of her down to the bed. "Everything I want for my birthday is right here on top of me," she said, as she reached down between her legs, spreading them apart and grabbing my penis and stroking it up and down at the same time rubbing it between her vagina.

I lifted my body in the air away from Medina's body with just my tongue circling her lips, bit her bottom lip and sucked it in my mouth. She was trying to pull me back down until I began running a straight line down her lips to her chin, down to her cleavage, palming her breast and sucked her left nipple in my mouth, then over to her right breast. I bit underneath her breast until it got cherry red, and both her nipples perked straight up in the air from the sting of my bite. I kept my body floating above hers and my tongue kept going down to her stomach where I licked her belly button. The further down I went, the more Medina's body began panting in anticipation of my tongue reaching her pubic hairs. Just beneath at her crown, I sucked on her clitoris. "Happy birthday," I said, sucking and pulling her clit between my lips as my tongue flicked at its tip. Medina grabbed my head with both hands the more I sucked and began to finger-fuck her at the same time.

"Oooooh yes," she exclaimed.

I worked my fingers in and out of her until my fingers were wet with thick creme running down her ass, and she began squeezing my head between her thighs as she was about to climax, and she began taking deep breaths that was followed by, "Oh Lord Jesus, yes oh yes!"

I fingered her in rapid motion then climbed on top of her and replaced my fingers with a deep long thrust of my penis. No words came out of Medina's mouth, she just had her mouth wide open and staring at me and I pounced in deep, pulled up leaving just the top of my head inside her core and began thrusting up and down, working from side to side. I lifted her legs up to my shoulders, reaching down to her hips and spreading her ass apart as I dug as deep inside of her wet pussy until it was gushy and so wet. Our fucking began to scent up the room and the sounds of slushing all drove my senses wild.

"Mmmmmm-um," I said as I could no longer hold back.

"Come with me," Medina said.

"I'm coming," I said.

"Right there, that's my spot!" she moaned.

We locked onto each other breathing harder until I was running out of blood to my brain, and oxygen to my lungs until I released inside of her, dropping all of my weight on top of her.

Medina lifted my head from her shoulder and filled my lips with several kisses. "That was an amazing surprise," she said. "I need more birthdays like that."

I smiled, then rolled off her and laid beside her. "Whoa," was all the verbiage I could say at the time.

We laid there fondling each other in full after-play and making new discoveries of each other's scars, moles, and dimples.

"Let's take a shower."

I looked over at the clock on the nightstand. Of the several hours Medina had demanded, six hours remained, so a shower was definitely needed.

"Alright, let's do it," I said after getting my heartbeat down to a normal pace.

"I'll go and get it nice and steamy," she said, jumping out of bed and heading into the bathroom.

I got up and followed Medina into the master bathroom where she was humming and fully lathered up in her birthday suit. I stepped inside the shower and took the foam sponge from her hand.

"So you're going to wash me up?" she asked.

"You deserve to be spoiled and pampered," I said and cleaned every part of her body that I planned to eat out, suck and stick my tongue in. Afterwards, Medina took a rag from the rack and scrubbed me clean, then turned around and took me inside of her as I pulled the shower head from its base and let the water-pick work her citrus, that drove her wild.

I almost had to carry Medina back into the bedroom after the fucking water-pick episode. We fell asleep in a naked embrace with scented Jasmine candles burning on the nightstands.

After an evening of hot steamy sex, a few hours of sleep and before the sun came up, I pulled the covers back and eased out of bed, got dressed and stood over Medina and admired the beautiful woman she is. On her nightstand was a pad and pen. I wrote, 'Happy Birthday and I hope to share many more to come.' I could not help thinking that I was always walking away from where I wanted to be in exchange for where I had to be.

Chapter
3

IN ORDER TO STAY ABREAST TO THE LATEST NEWS, most people tune into the morning news for the weather, stock, and current events. My daily briefings started by receiving or calling Castro, and as soon as I left Medina's house and my wheels were turning up the highway, that's exactly what I did.

"Hello," I said into the phone after two rings and Castro picked up.

"Where you at?" he asked in an aggressive tone.

"Headed your way, what's up?"

"I'll tell you when you get here."

"Alright, I'll be pulling up in about fifteen minutes."

"Yep," he said, then ended the call.

The morning news never waits and since Castro was delaying his response to my inquiry, I could sense something had occurred overnight and that was the reason for his morning aggression. That and the fact he requested a thousand times that I stopped allowing Medina to turn my phone off whenever I was out of reach.

Castro lived in Southfield, Michigan and was southbound coming from Medina's house heading back into the city. So, whatever it was he had to tell me, I'd know in a matter of minutes. We stuck to the O.G. rules and never discussed important business over the phone. I sped up just to cut my time short because I knew it was going to be a long morning when things were already getting in the way of my plans. I had to have a sit-down with Andrew Valentino, my supplier that he requested. The old man had better ears to the streets than I had boots on the ground. A sudden call from Mr. Valentino always made me pick the phone up to double check with Castro to be sure there wasn't anything moving on the streets that I did not know about which I should know about. The last thing I wanted to do was to be sitting across from the old man who brought me into the game looking like I was still wet behind the ears.

I came off the Southfield Freeway looking in my rearview mirror thinking about the GTO and regretting I was unable to get the plate numbers which made it senseless to bring up to Castro without having any leads for him to look into.

He was standing out front of his house smoking a cigarette when I pulled up. He thumped the cigarette into the street and headed for the passenger's door as soon as I turned into his driveway, jumped inside to lock the winter chill outside.

"Man, its colder than a motherfucker," he said, then putting his hands up to the vents to warm them up. "What's up with you?" he asked.

"I'll know that when you tell me what's going on."

"Man, they did it," Castro pounded the air with his fist. "Those punk motherfuckahs actually did that shit."

I didn't know if he was talking to me or to himself by the way he was looking out the window as if still processing whatever it was they had done to himself.

"You look awfully calm," he said looking over at me. "What, you get some pussy last night?"

"You haven't given me a reason why I should not be calm," I said. "So, what's up?"

"Well, whatever you got into I hope it was worth it because you may not be getting any for a while," he said. "Those crazy motherfuckin' Rakehells decided to send the families their calling card last night. Those bitch ass motherfuckers shot up the Brotherhood."

"Are you sure?" I asked. "That doesn't make sense."

"Yeah, like what have they done these past six months make any sense?"

"And this happened last night?"

"Check your messages man, I called you as soon as they did the shit."

"I got your message."

"No, the fuck you didn't or you would have picked up your phone," he said. "I'm sure you got it right before you headed this way a few minutes ago. I told you about that disappearing pussy stunts you be pulling where nobody knows how to reach you ain't cool."

While Castro was ranting about my nightlife, I was piecing together the timelines between when the Rakehells shot up the

Brotherhood and the call I got from Mr. Valentino wanting to meet.

"So how do we know it was Rakehell?" I asked.

"We know because they never got pass security in the parking lot or pass the bouncer at the door."

"Were any of our moonlighting cops involved?"

"Lion, them boys deserve a bonus because the moonlighters worked inside the club and what went on outside never made it inside."

"We lose any people?"

"It wasn't our detail last night so our shit is intact, but four were lost all together."

"Have we reached out to their families?"

"All that shaking hands and shit is your thing," he said, "but the old man called asking about you."

"The old man called you?"

"Yeah, ain't that some shit. I didn't even know he had my number. But he did not sound too happy, said y'all had a meeting."

"That's all he said?"

"The man doesn't have to say anything, just him calling says everything." He went in his pocket, "Here, he said to give you this and wanted you at his house as soon as you got the message."

"Okay," I said, looking at the address. "Line a meeting up with the Tokyo Twins."

"You gonna bring them in on this?"

"I think they'll be helpful."

"Yeah I agree."

"I'll call you after I'm done with the old man."

"Yep," Castro said, getting out of the car and closing the door.

I looked at my watch thinking I had put Mr. Valentino's request for a meeting off long enough. Although the Legion family were old school and the weakest of all the families, they were always the most demanding and had the highest opinions to put before the committee.

I backed out of Castro's driveway with him standing there lighting up another cigarette, appearing to be consumed by his own thoughts and before I could make it to the corner of his block, my phone rang.

"Lion speaking," I said into the car speakers.

"Did you get my message?" the scratchy voice of Mr. Valentino asked.

"Just now," I replied.

"When can you be here?"

"Twenty minutes."

That's all that was said and we both hung up. Mr. Valentino had no muscle on the streets, which is where the Lion family came in, but he supplied the upper north region of Ohio, Chicago, and Michigan. That was his muscle because if he chose to cut off our supply, then there was no one else that could mass distribute on that scale. So, him calling for a meeting was a big deal.

There was no morning rush hour traffic so I was able to keep my timing at the twenty minutes that I said it would take for me to get there. Beverly Hills, Michigan was upper crust and every mansion I passed looked like money, and there was a difference in old money versus big new faces. New money was loud and arrogant while old money is reserved and subtle.

Chapter
4

THERE WAS SECURITY CAMERA AIMED AT THE FRONT GATE, and I could only assume I was being watched because the gate began to open just as a well-dressed gentleman was walking out of the front door heading towards me. By the time the gate was in a locked back position, he was peering inside of my window over the top of his dark shades as I lowered my window.

"Can I help you?" the well-dressed Italian asked.

"Yeah, sure," I said to play his game. I was pretty sure he wasn't in the business of opening gates with a stranger out front. "I'm here to see Mr. Valentino."

"And who may I tell him is calling?"

I didn't say anything at first. For some reason, I felt contempt for Andrew's grease ball to be addressing me as if I was showing up to his home, as if I was a lost soul looking for directions. Especially since he had called the meeting, followed by his call to Castro to come see him asap.

"Lion," I finally said. "Tell him, Lion is here."

He smiled, "Pleased to meet you, Mr. Lion."

I did not know what to make of his smile, so I didn't return it.

"You can park anywhere out front here," he said, pointing up the driveway and stepping off to the side.

He met me once I'd parked and we both entered the lavish home. "I'll let Mr. Valentino know you're here," he said, leaving me standing at the entrance of the spacious foyer.

"Oh, hello!" A beautiful spa-tanned long haired brunette woman said as she spun her head around to my presence and came to an abrupt halt, turned in my direction and headed towards me, flipping her hair over her shoulder, and locking it behind her ear. "I'm Ferrell Valentino," she said with a perfectly leveled smile and her hand extended out for a handshake by the time she was standing in front of me. "You must be our Lion."

"I am, The Lion," I said, taking her hand into my hand, "and it's a pleasure to meet you Mrs. Valentino."

She maintained her smile over being corrected with a slight squinting of her brown eyes.

"It fits you very nicely," she said.

"Thank you," I responded, while letting go of her hand and straightening my suit lapel.

She giggled. "That too, but I was talking about your name."

"As does yours," I smiled.

A curious look came over her eyes.

"Would that be the dress or my name, Mr. Lion?"

"Well, since you already know what that dress does for you,

or you wouldn't have chosen to wear it, I'll just stay on the safe side of the Mister and stick with the name."

Ferrell, was wearing a three-quarter length tightly woven button down one piece and had left the top four button holes unlocked, leaving plenty of room for cleave exposure. The dress, her eyeliner and glossy red cherry-colored lips were in perfect formation.

"Care to join me?" she asked.

"I would be delighted but I'm here on business."

"And he has you waiting, right?"

"Yes."

"Then he won't mind me keeping you company until he comes down." She turned her back to me, then twisted half around and with her French manicured candy-pink fingernail, gestured in a follow-me motion, saying, "This way, Mr. Lion."

I followed behind the scent of her Dolce & Gabbana perfume thinking that she was a natural coquette. Her long hair flowed to the midsection of her back, drawing my attention to her tail feather, that I gave a perfect ten.

"This will give you the entire view of the back," she said, turning around to see that I was already enjoying the view. But she was referring to the golf course that served as their backyard from the open picture window in the parlor.

"Very nice," I complimented.

"You should see it when the grounds are fertile and the rabbits are running wild," she laughed. "It's such a sight to experience. Please, have a seat."

I started to sit down on the sofa.

"No, why don't you sit over here. That way, we won't have to strain our voices to communicate."

I took a seat on one of the twin chairs next to Ferrell, close to the picture window where a coffee table stood between us with a tray on it where she must had already been having her noon tea.

"I'm having tea. Would you like to join me, or can I entice you to something else?" she propositioned, pouring herself a cup from a sterling silver long snout.

"Tea will be fine," I said.

"Sugar or lemon?"

"Sugar."

"You know I've been waiting to meet you, seems like forever. How many?"

"Two, and is that a fact?"

"Yes," she said while handing me the cup of tea. "You're like a household name around here." She paused, "Yes David, what is it?"

The suit that met me at the entrance had a name, David. And he was standing in the doorway with a bleak look on his face. I looked over at him wondering how long he had been standing there ear hustling our conversation.

"I was instructed to take Mr. Lion into Mr. Valentino's office," he said to her without taking his eyes off of me.

"Tell Andrew we're having tea in the parlor."

There's one thing absolute in the animal kingdom of nature, and it's evident when a pecking order must be established. David and I were like the lion versus the hyena with the scent of a fresh kill in the air. But, unlike me, he held his dislike behind dark shades while I was capable of looking any man directly in the eyes and let him know just where he stood with me, win, lose, or draw. He stood there in the doorway as tense as a gazelle contemplating his fight or flight options. But no matter how many deer heads, boars, and taxidermy wildlife hung from the walls of their estate, he wasn't the hunter I was, and it was only because I was in his home that I allowed his aggressive stares to continue as far as they had. He lived a lavish lifestyle from a suburban retreat far away from people like me who was now sitting in his home.

"That will be all, David," Ferrell said in a definite tone, followed by, "and please close the door behind you."

I could have laughed in David's face but I held it inside.

"Now, where were we?" she asked with her eyes glued on David until he was out of sight behind the closed door.

"Our meeting," I nudged her memory.

"Oh yes," she said, sipped her tea and placed it back on the saucer. "We — you and I — share more than you realize Mr. Lion."

"Lion, why don't you call me Lion, Mrs. Valentino."

"Why don't you call me, Ferrell," she said, "and it's not Mrs."

"You're not?"

I was a little thrilled to know I had not been flirting with a married woman, then noted no bling-bling wedding ring.

She laughed. "No, Andrew is my brother."

"So you're the well-kept secret he protects."

"I'm not as much a secret as you think, Lion. You've just been hanging in the wrong places."

"Yeah, well I don't belong to any country clubs, and I damn sure don't play golf. But I'm open to making a few changes in your case."

"You won't have to if you make yourself available."

"I'm here, aren't I?"

"I mean aside from a business call, where we can become more acquainted."

"Careful Ferrell, I might call you out on that."

"Call me out, really?"

"Yeah, to back your words up with your action."

"Oh, and what makes you think volleying isn't a warm up for action?" she asked, crossing her legs, allowing the fullness of her thigh to show where the buttons of her dress met as she leaned towards me and halfway out of the chair.

"I think you're a very beautiful woman who plays by your own rules."

"Meaning?"

"Meaning, nothing. Forget I said that."

I thought I'd better back off a little before things got out of control. Ferrell came across as the daring type and would do or say a thing because she was warned against it. Like most women who always wanted what they felt they could not fully possess.

"Come on Lion! We're adults here, you're so interesting and a great conversationalist. Now tell me what you were about to say."

For a few tense moments we held a deep eye contact.

"That's what I'm saying right there," I said.

"What?" She blushed.

"I'm your forbidden fruit and a danger that represents a thrill for you. But what you don't realize is I'm like a drug, an addictive drug that you won't just shake cold turkey."

"You're so full of yourself. Oh my god!" She laughed.

Ferrell was laughing but the chemistry in the room bounced off the walls reflected by the gaze in her almond shaped eyes that she could not conceal from detection. She may have been skilled at volleying, but her body language spoke beyond her words.

"And what about you, can you play on unfamiliar grounds out in the wild?"

She pushed her hair behind her left ear and fixed her seductive eyes on me.

"How wild can you handle it?"

That is how it should read, but the word "side" is missing, and the sentence is all scrambled up and makes no since. I motioned to get up to meet him.

"No, no-no, sit, sit," he said with David following behind him. "Leave us alone, David," he ordered.

David left in the same snail's pace as he had when Ferrell had dismissed him from the room, but leaving the door ajar.

Mr. Valentino, sat down on the sofa with all the ease of aging bones slowing the bend, releasing a loud grunt as the seat comforted him.

"How are you, old friend? I see you and Ferrell saved me from having to make an introduction between the two of you."

"Yes, we've met," I said, looking at him and then at Ferrell, who seemed to smile naturally.

I had sensed the meeting was more than I had anticipated.

"A testy one, isn't she?" he asked.

"Great spirit, yes she is."

"How much has she told you?"

"About what?"

"I haven't told Lion, anything Andrew," she interjected. "We were waiting on you."

He looked at the both of us, then said, "Seeing you two sitting there together is almost scary."

"Please don't start, Andrew," Ferrell appealed.

"The man has the right to know what he's being involved in."

"I think Lion can handle himself very well."

"It's not him I'm worried about, but the two of you together," Andrew said while pointing his nervous finger in the air and waived it from side to side, "will be a marriage of the highest order."

I was contented to sit on the sidelines observing the sister/brother fencing until the word 'marriage' was thrown across the battle lines aiming directly at me.

"Excuse me, Mr. Valentino, but did I just hear marriage mentioned?"

They both laughed.

"You better stop fooling around Andrew, and let him know why he's here."

"Oh, for heaven's sake! Must you two always be so damn serious?"

"Just tell him."

"Tell me what?"

"Okay," Andrew relented.

Looking over at Ferrell, I could surmise her impatience for Andrew to reveal the purpose of our meeting.

"I've heard about the Brotherhood situation but I won't ask you if I should be concerned and I'm sure it will be resolved discreetly."

"What problem?" I asked.

He shook his head in agreement. "Exactly."

I looked over at Ferrell, then at him.

"Don't worry about her, she knows more about what's going on. Time will reveal. You will have plenty of time to compare notes."

"How's that?"

"Lion, I'm the last of the male Valentino's. And since Ferrell refuses to produce any males to take my place, she's in line to run the family operation."

There it was out in the open. I sat back in my seat, but I still tried to sit back further.

"So, you're out?" I asked.

He shook his head up and down. "As of today, the marriage of the Legion family and the Lion family will consist of you two's relationship. I'm an old man now and I've become too absent minded to keep this business up. Ferrell had played the shadows for a few years now running things while I took the credit. It's her time to lead the family. This business has gotten too ugly for me, and I just don't have the strength to read the papers anymore. I'll be moving to Florida, getting the hell away from this cold climate and resting my bones in the sun."

Ferrell, sat in silence looking at the both of us. Her smile removed as the tone of the meeting had turned deadly serious and her blood brother was asking me to fill his shoes in looking after his sister so that he could find an easy tree to rest under after a long life of fast money, death and drugs shipped into the United States by the tons.

"She's a wild tiger, Lion." He touched my hand. "But she doesn't know enough about the streets to do this without some muscle to keep her guarded."

I stood up and so did he, looking each other square in the eyes and I said, "You have my dying declaration that I will protect Ferrell Valentino, even if it costs me my own life and those under my command."

Without words, he unbuttoned his shirt and removed a gold chain from his neck that held the Legion family ring. "It should fit."

"I can't take your ring, Mr. Valentino," I said.

"Go ahead, take it," he insisted.

"I don't know what to say."

"Why don't you start by taking Ferrell, for a celebration."

That was how Mr. Valentino and my relationship ended and Ferrell's and I began. The ring was a symbolic transfer of power, the vows an allegiance till dope do us part.

Chapter
5

THE SCENT OF A WOMAN IS LIKE A FINGERPRINT — unique and stimulating. And once she has rubbed her natural body odor or perfume across your senses, it is something that will stay with you for life. The most popular perfume in the world may have been created by Dolce & Gabbana, but the first woman you ever smell it on will forever rule over your thoughts of her. Even if it is worn by another woman.

Ferrell was a stunningly beautiful woman. I had no idea if she had other plans before my arrival, but I was pleased that she had decided to change into something that would draw a little less attention, if that was actually possible. She had changed into a pair of designer jeans that hugged her curves, a traditional holiday sweater, Divine Diva bomber jacket, and a pair of Uggs boots. It's impossible to downplay natural beauty, but flashy can draw unnecessary attention when you're trying to get in and out of places without being remembered as much.

I opened the passenger's door for her. "Thank you," she said, climbing inside and began putting on her seatbelt as I closed the door and walked around to the other side where she had already leaned over and opened my door. I got in and as soon as I turned the ignition over, the music took over the interior of the car.

Nothing was said while the music played, and we got onto the highway heading towards Lenox Township. I had already received a text message from Castro saying the Tokyo Twins would be expecting my arrival.

"She's nice," Ferrell said, breaking the silence. "Who is she?"

I turned the volume down. "Her," I said. "Her?"

"Yeah but its capital H.E.R."

"You have not spoken a word since we left the house. Has all of this upset you?"

"I was more or less thinking about how I underestimated you back there."

"What do you mean?"

"I think you know what I mean. You let me come in there knowing all along why I was there and you —""Took advantage of you?" Ferrell interjected.

I just smiled.

"Come one Lion, now we both know that all is fair in love and war. Yes, I did know why you were there but it's nothing like what you're thinking."

"Then what should I be thinking?"

"We were fencing and establishing our ground."

"Without me knowing stakes or the rules to the game."

"Come on, I think for someone who did not know the stakes,

you came equipped to deal with whatever came your way. What is it, you don't like being married to me?"

"We're not married."

Ferrell snickered. "Oh, that's funny?"

"You know what's funny to me is you've been married to Andrew and the Legion family, for how many years? And now here you are reluctant to enter marriage with the family's First Lady."

"You make it sound like I was laying Andrew."

"You know what I mean, and I did not say you had to sleep with me... yet," she added jokingly.

Or at least I thought she may have been joking.

"Does that come with the marriage?" I asked, coming up off the expressway, taking Gratiot Avenue down to Haven Road.

Ferrell brushed the curls of her hair over her shoulder, then twisting her head slightly sideways as if to study me before she responded, and looked out of the passenger's window clearing her throat before looking at me with flushed cheeks.

"Is that a yes?" I pressed her.

"Do you want it to?" she asked.

"Do you think that would be wise?"

"You're The Lion," she said with emphasis, "and we're two consenting adults."

"What if I said I have a woman?"

"What if I said what's your business is your business and what goes on between us is our business?"

"And you think you can handle that?"

"Marriages fail when the rules of engagement aren't laid out from the start and maintained."

I laughed. "I've heard that before."

"But you never heard it coming from me."

I turned into the Macomb County Township condo's parking lot and backed the Jaguar into the first available parking space I saw and turned off the engine.

"What makes you think you're any different from all other women?" I asked.

"First of all," she started, "I'm not after your money so you can rest assured that that's not my objective. And second, I'm willing to do whatever it takes to make this marriage of our families work to our mutual benefits. So, whether you put your ring on or not, I know you're a man of your word and wouldn't have accepted the offer if you did not plan to honor your word. And for those reasons, I'm prepared to be to you what no other women can ever be to you nor have ever been there for you as I will."

I got out of the car processing Ferrell's words, felt the ring in my pocket as I walked around and opened her door.

"This is where you live?" she asked as she took my hand and got out of the car.

"No," I said. "The Tokyo Twins live here."

"Andrew has mentioned them, very ambitious."

"Those are kind words."

I pushed the door buzzer to the Tokyo Twins' condo and were let in by a loud buzz which unlocked the all-glass door.

"They're beautiful," Ferrell said, as we looked up the hallway to where they were standing and waiting to greet us.

"The deadliest kind," I mumbled beneath my breath.

As the Legion families First Lady, this was where Ferrell got her feet wet in rubbing shoulders with other women whose deadly venom she would have to eventually match in order to survive in the cartel.

Chapter 6

DELICATE AS PORCELAIN DOLLS YET DEADLY AS TWIN bites from a king cobra. Sometimes the best thing you can do is warn someone of pending danger; how they approach it afterwards is playing at their own risk.

"Ladies," I said upon approaching the twins.

"Hello Lion," they said almost at the same time.

"Please come in."

"Thank you," I said. No matter how hard I tried to find something that separated the twins, it was impossible. Aside from meeting them and one having her hair done slightly different or a piece of jewelry, but that only lasted for the moment. The next time we met, I had to do the same thing. So I never called them by their names until I found that one distinguishing thing that set them apart.

There was immediate tension in the air by the second twin who did not take her eyes off Ferrell for a second as we entered the apartment.

"I want to introduce you to the First Lady, Miss Valentino," I said to the both but mainly to twin number two.

"These are the Tokyo Twins," I introduced them.

"Hello Miss Valentino, I'm Ninon," the outspoken one said, "but everyone calls me Nin.

It was the first time Ferrell let go of my arm and I took a step back as they shook hands.

"Why don't we have a seat," Nin offered, leading the way.

The main room which typically serves as a living room had been turned into a conference room, full length table and leather chairs, and a large conference screen for Skype calls.

We sat down mid-center on both sides, the twins on one side and Ferrell sat next to me. I sat there as the women exchanged pleasantries and the second twin lightened her aggressiveness just a bit to be sociable.

"Anyway," Ferrell finally said as she reached over and touched my hand that was resting on the armchair, "I'm sure Lion wants to get down to business."

"Thank you Ms. Valentino," I said, "and I'll try to be brief."

"Well, we'll help you out Lion," Nin said. "We already have the details concerning the Brotherhood and the Rakehell family's show of disrespect."

"That's good," I said. "So, the only one here who isn't fully briefed is Ms. Valentino. But she's here with me because I wanted you two to be the first to know that she will be our supplier now that her brother has retired."

I turned my attention to Ferrell. "The Rakehell family has or had a seat at the table but due to their obsessive violent tendencies, they were fined and suspended from the table for one hundred and eighty days. Oddly they decided, one week from completing their sanctions to shoot up the Brotherhood Club, the one place no family is allowed to bring harm to any other family that has a seat at the table."

"I see," Ferrell said.

I continued, "Unfortunately for them, they chose the route that we will not turn the other cheek and let the dust settle. And not to belittle anyone's intelligence but Rakehell means, 'one who rakes the coals of hell,' and that's where their family will be driven back to — hell." I turned to the twins, "And this is where your services will be required and most valuable because the Rakehell's will be on the ready for our response. We know of all the families, your family is the only one they will trust to get close enough to them to draw them out into the opening."

Ninon sat back in her chair. "Madame Cordelia," she said.

"You're the only one she'll agree to talk to," I said. "My sergeant-at-arms, Blast, will be in charge of the Crazy-Eight, and they will take their orders from Castro. But this is not an order I'm issuing so much as it's an opportunity you Nin, and you Ninon to expand your territory. For your participation, you will have my vote at the table to take over the Rakehell's region, and since I'm the chairman and break all tie votes, I can almost guarantee you the zone will be yours."

I paused.

"Well, if you don't mind me weighing in," Ninon said, "because we already have an obligation being at the table to respond to the assault by Rakehell, you've just given us a bonus reason to taking point." She smiled, "To be awarded Madame Cordelia's zone, we will deliver her head on a silver platter to the Brotherhood's table."

"Then it's agreed?"

"Under one condition," Ninon said.

"And what's that?" I asked, hoping I wouldn't regret it.

"We've never worked together as a team, but we've heard a great deal about the method and tactics of your Crazy-Eight."

"Mmm.""They have a take-no-prisoners approach and we just need assurance and because it's well known that we have history with the Rakehells, that the Crazy-Eight don't come in with guns-a-blazing, because with all due respect, I'm a little paranoid to be sharing the battlefield with a psycho crew."

"I can assure you the Crazy-Eight are very disciplined when it comes to their executions, and what they do is supposed to be brutal when the civil side of negotiations fail."

"I don't know if that's supposed to put us at ease or what but I'll take it as an agreement," Ninon said.

"That said," I stood from my chair, "I have another meeting that requires my presence. Ladies, I look forward to seeing this to a close."

Ferrell stood up beside me, "It was... I guess nice to meet the two of you."

They looked at each other and laughed.

"I wish it could have been on different terms as well, Ms. Valentino," Nin said.

"Please, call me Ferrell," she said, reaching across the table and they shook hands.

"I will, Ferrell."

"Nin," Ferrell said and they shook hands as well.

"We look forward to working with you Ferrell-l-l," Nin said, adding a few syllables to her name.

The Tokyo Twins escorted us to the door and I still didn't know which was which although Ferrell seem to shake the right hands when acknowledging them.

Chapter 7

THE KILLER INSTINCT INSIDE ALL OF US CAN LAY DORMANT our entire lives, yet all it takes is a split second, crisis, or threat to resurrect that survival instinct. Some are fortunate enough to go a lifetime without that Sphinx being awakened while others are tested to that breaking point of fight or flight.

The convenience for most people who never reach this self-awareness are those who hide behind the 911 emergency contact as opposed to those who stop running, turn around, and face the lion chasing you that is self. When that is done, nothing outside of self can defeat you.

"That was interesting," Ferrell said after we'd left the Tokyo Twins and was on 94 Expressway. I knew the meeting was a lot to process so I allowed her the space she needed to come to her own conclusions.

"The rapper 2Pac or our meeting?" I asked, which was the artist I had just turned on.

"I've heard of him but not, you know, with all the profanity. He sounds so angry."

"He was."

"He's dead?"

I laughed. "Kind of, yes."

"What does that mean, he can't be kind of dead."

"I'll be a legend breathing or dead, was one of his famous lines," I said, "But I don't think you really want to talk about a dead rapper."

I took Grosse Pointe to Kercheval street on the east side of Detroit.

"Oh sorry," she said.

"Sorry for what?"

"I don't know, I just thought this may be a touchy subject for you."

I laughed. "You know you're taking advantage of me."

"How so?"

"Because I see your capable of tuning things out. One second, you seemed compassionate and caring and the next you're ice-cold. Like back there with the twins where you've ordered the deaths of an entire family in a manner which for me caused the room to spin, and those women as beautiful as they are seemed to have no problem allowing you to lead them to death's door."

I pulled into my driveway and turned the engine off, killing the last words of "Heartz of Men" by 2Pac. "We're going to have to talk about this later because I have to be somewhere else right now." I opened my door and got out.

Ferrell did not move.

"Let's go," I said from in front of the car looking back at her.

She got out and slammed my car door with all of her attitude.

⟨⟨⟨⟩⟩⟩

"This is your home?" she asked, standing behind me as I unlocked the door.

"Yeah," I said after opening the door, stepping inside and holding it open for her to come in, then closed it.

"This is nice, but why can't we talk about the meeting?"

"Good, I'm glad you like it so you won't mind making yourself comfortable until I get back."

"Wait-what?"

"You'll find everything you need. It's not as big as your mansion but all of the amenities are here," I said, walking beside her into the living room. "No one will bother you and there's plenty of food as well as a fully stocked bar, and if you go for smoking, there's a cigar case on the bar with wood blunts. I'll be back in a couple of hours max."

"Can you do this?? I mean I know you can but why can't I come with you?"

"Because this is a personal matter I have to deal with and you live too far away for me to take you home, so this will have to do for now."

Ferrell stood in the middle of the floor, folded her arms and looked around as if weighing her options before locking her brown eyes on to me.

I turned to walk out and she rushed over and grabbed my

arm, "You're not going to go after those people right now, are you? I mean… are you?"

"No, I have to see a family member," I said as she let go of my arm. "You can lock the door if it makes you feel safer."

"Okay," she said, following me to the door, "but I don't understand when you're talking about family-business or family-blood."

Ferrell stood in the door until I backed out of the driveway, and I had to contend with the mix of family-blood business.

Chapter
8

ROSA PARKS BOULEVARD & GLADSTONE WAS ON THE westside of Detroit.

Pharaoh lived in the two-family flat off the corner that had been converted into a single resident. He and I were as close as any family could ever be, and he was the only person I knew would cut a dime in half to give me a nickel if I was broke. That was before I made a name for myself, which I never forgot during my climb to power. No matter what I had going on in the run of a day, I always made time to drop in on him and to make sure he did not need for anything I had the power to provide, which did not go unnoticed by our family.

Pharaoh had his demons which was the one thing I could not save him from — that dreadful needle. I used his upstairs kitchen to turn powder cocaine into rocks. He was always happy to see me because he knew I was going to hook him up without question. Later he began telling me about a cheap form of heroin called "mixjive" and how I should invest in the product.

I later made a small investment when he proposed he'd run the operation if I did. It put him in the position of being his own best customer, but it also turned out to be very lucrative, like ten grand before noon, lucrative. "I told you, boy!" he laughed the first day he called me after selling out of the product. What was a well-kept secret was that Pharaoh had been diagnosed with cancer, and aside from having no insurance, there was nothing the doctors could do to help him. The drugs were a way of self-medicating his pain away and replaced the medical coverage he couldn't afford. This was a secret that he held close to the vest and despite his rapid weight loss, no one seemed concerned about his physical wellbeing.

I pulled up next to Jesse, who was parked several houses away from Pharaoh's place.

"Jesse," I said after lowering my window, "everything good?"

"Same dog, different day," he responded. "Where's yo shadow?"

"About fifteen minutes out."

"I'll just squat until he is on deck," he said.

I nodded approval and pulled off. Before I could park, the front door was opening. The lookout man had signaled the door man that I was there.

"What's going on in here?" I said, stepping inside the door as it was immediately slammed shut and locked behind me.

"What's happening, Lion?" one of the addicts said with an intoxicated grin.

"Where's Pharaoh?" I asked, taking a seat on the sofa, and looking at my watch.

Just then he walked into the living room drying his hands with a paper napkin. "What's up boyyyy?" he said, always happy to see me.

I touched my watch. "Where's your man?" I asked him.

"Shorty, have a seat man or go clean another room," he said to the junky who couldn't sit still. "I just got off the phone with him five minutes ago. He should be here soon, you hungry?"

"No, I'm good."

He looked out of the corner of the window before sitting down himself. Before he could get comfortable, the doorman let him know we had company.

"It's your man," he said.

"What's up, Chuck?" I asked as he walked into the room.

"Shit, what's happening with you?" he said, greeting Pharaoh with a handshake. "I heard about that bullshit at the hood."

"Castro will plug you on it later," I said. "He's taking point."

Within a few moments of everyone settling in, the house began to tremble like an earthquake had hit it. I looked around to see if I was the only one having the experience.

"That'll be Milton," Pharaoh said as if he needed to be announced.

"What is he driving, a fucking tractor?" I asked. "Not only does he show up late, but he informs the entire neighborhood as well."

Pharaoh got up and rushed to the door to meet this Milton character.

"My bad," he apologized. "My muffler fell on the way here."

The exchange was quick. Chuck tested the product that would come to be known as "Earthquake".

I stood up and told Pharaoh, "Call me if you need me."

"Alright boyyy," he said. "Be safe out there.

Chuck and I parted ways after leaving the house, and I descended the steps overhearing Pharaoh barking orders to those who would do anything to be in his good graces. All money ain't good money, sometimes it's just simply survival, and I just didn't want to see him going out suffering in enormous pain.

Chapter 9

SEEING PHARAOH IN HIS FRAIL CONDITION ALWAYS LEFT ME IN A TRANCE, and before I knew it, I was back in my Grosse Pointe driveway where I had left Ferrell. I decided to put the car in the garage and take the back entrance into the house.

"Oh shit!" Ferrell said, grabbing her chest. "You scared me. I did not hear you come in."

"I came in through the back," I said, walking into the living room, noticing she had lit the fireplace. I took a cigar from its box atop the fireplace, lit it from the fire, and sat down to watch the dancing flames.

Her eyes were glued onto my every move. "I didn't know you smoked."

"There's a lot of things about me you don't know," I said, blowing a cloud of gray smoke towards the flames.

"I know you're slow to anger, but once you're there it's intense."

"So we're back to that, huh?"

"It's just the third time tonight I've seen you upset."

I did not respond.

"Is it something I've done?" she pressed me.

"It has nothing to do with you."

"Oh," she said with a calm smile. "Do you always shut everyone out when you're upset?"

"Who said I was upset?"

"Your nostrils," she said. "You know I've never sat across from you until today to observe your physical being in motion, but from the many conversations I've had with Andrew, I feel as if this moment is just bringing all of you into focus."

Ferrell was not like most women I'd known who would have either sat there in silence, gave me space, or avoided the issue. She just sat there trying to calm my mind and get to the root of my anger.

"Is this why you left me here alone?"

"What?"

"Wherever it was you went. I mean earlier you were able to mask your emotions behind your anger. But now it's deeper. Is that why you would not take me with you?"

"Am I being psychologically analyzed?"

She blushed, then I laughed.

"There, right there. That's what I'm talking about."

"What are you talking about?"

"You're such a handsome, masculine, dark complexioned man. But there's so much more to it. What perplexes me is how you're able to turn a smile upside down like a switch. You came in here almost looking like you could kill me, making me afraid and now you sit there with a smile as warm as those flames as if nothing in the world can get beneath your skin. Is it a Lion thing that prevents you from expressing your other emotions?"

"Life doesn't afford us such freedom of expressions."

"Says who?"

"It's an unwritten rule, but enough about me," I said, stubbing the cigar out in the ashtray. "I know why Andrew wants me to wear the Legion family ring. What I want to know is why you chose me to wear it and not David, because from what I gathered at the house, you've been the button pusher for a while now, and why this profession?"

"You wouldn't believe me if I told you."

"Try me."

"Okay I'll try you," she said. "It was you."

"Me?" I pointed at myself, puzzled.

"Yes, but I'm sure although it may come as a surprise, it's not new to you to see others aspire to live up to your standards."

"In the hood, there are guys that style themselves after my reputation but you just met me today."

"No, I'm just meeting you in person today, but I've known of you ever since you got your first bag from Andrew. He was so impressed with your style until he could not stop talking about you. Every day it was Lion this and Lion that, so much so that I hated hearing your name. David was the same way; we both counted the minutes between how many times Andrew would say your name. David actually admires you also, but hates you because Andrew would never let him forget why he could never be a take charge person like, Lion."

This was the first time I had any knowledge Mr. Valentino thought so highly of me.

"Anyway," Ferrell continued, "I think seeing how much it got under David's nails, I began to realize you're shrinking any chances he had of wearing the family ring. Eventually I began to look forward to Andrew talking about you and later started asking questions of my own about you. For example, I know all about where it is you go when you come back like you've done this evening. Andrew knows as well but never wanted to meddle around in your personal affairs. He wanted to help but didn't know how he could without letting on that he was keeping tabs on your every move."

"Really?"

"It wasn't that he didn't trust you, maybe at first, but I think he stumbled upon this information because he was considering you long before we both actually openly aired our thoughts of passing the Legion family ring over to you for consideration. Andrew was actually brought to tears when your secret was revealed to him and said the single greatest thing you've done is your greatest secret. And because I had never seen anyone move him in such a way, something inside of me wanted to be closer to you and the only way that could be made possible was for me to take over the family business."

"You couldn't have just asked him to introduce us?"

"I did but he flatly refused, saying he would not do so under such conditions because you were too dangerous and too valuable for me to get involved in family affairs for social reasons."

"And you chose the most dangerous profession on earth just to meet me?"

"I told you, you wouldn't believe me."

I did not know if Ferrell was insane or was one of those fatal attraction type women who wanted what she wanted and would do anything to get what she wanted. I had gone out of my way to impress a woman I wanted to get close to before but never to this degree.

"So you see," she said, "I wasn't taking advantage of you at the house. The excitement of finally meeting you overwhelmed me a bit, but it was sincere."

"I see," I said. "I think we ought to get you home before Andrew puts an APB out for you."

"Why? Was I too honest and you need time to process everything I've said?"

"It's a lot to digest, but that's not it."

"I'm not ever going to lie to you, Lion."

"Well, I hope not because looks like we're going to be spending a lot of time together."

"There's something else I need to tell you."

"Okay, what is it?"

"Andrew's gone," she said. "He left for Florida, not long after we left the house."

"Did you know he was planning to leave today?"

"Yes."

"Wait a minute. Are you telling me that you knew he was leaving the State and you chose to follow me around instead of staying with him? And what do you mean no one is there? What about David, he went with Andrew?"

"Yes, yes and yes," she said.

I laughed and shook my head in disbelief.

"What's wrong?"

"So, you're here alone now?"

"No, I'm not alone."

"You lost me."

"I have you."

"Me, you have me?"

"What part of accepting that ring from Andrew you didn't understand, Lion?"

"Don't try to fuckin' drill me! Your only family has dropped a ring in my hand, and you on my doorstep and skipped town in the same hour and you're going to sit there like this is business as usual. So, when were you planning to tell me guarding you started?"

"Andrew was out of the picture the fuckin' very second you let that ring fall into your hand, and you started guarding me the minute you pledged your life and the life of those under your command. You're not the one green here, so you know this business far better than I do so don't act like you're surprised that I'm at your mercy. So now that you know you're the boss, or at least until I'm able to hold my own, let's try to establish some ground rules. This has not been an easy thing for me to adjust to, but I have my big girl panties and now is not the time for you to turn your anger on me."

"You'll be taking the guest room," I said, getting up and

heading for my bedroom as Ferrell stood up and followed behind me.

"Is that all you have to say?" she asked as I pushed the guest door open.

"Everything is fresh, and you'll have to use one of my shirts to sleep in," I said, feeling like we were a couple having our first fight.

"Muthfuckah," I said as I sat on the edge of my bed in my boxers, thinking about my predicament. No doubt I had accepted the ring from Mr. Valentino, so Ferrell was in and there wasn't anything I could do to change that.

The ring, I thought. I had left it in the living room on the coffee table and thought about the rules Ferrell suggested we needed to establish. I went in the living room, stood there in my boxers looking down at the ring, wondering for the first time, how much power came with its ownership. I picked it up for close examination, opened the cigar box, took out a cigar and slid the ring onto it, placed it back into the box and slammed it shut.

Ferrell had left the guest door open. She was under the spread with her back to the door and refused to turn over when I entered the room and sat in the chair at the foot of the bed.

"Are you just going to sit there watching over me all night?" she asked without lifting her head from the pillow.

"About those rules," I said.

The question caused her to turn over and sit up in the bed. The cover fell to her waist exposing her perky breast by the dim hallway light.

"Where do we start?" she asked.

"Trusting in each other."

"How do we get there?"

"Do you trust me?"

"I'm here fully exposed in front of you, isn't that a good start?"

"Do you trust me to know your deepest secrets?"

Ferrell pushed her hair back from covering her left eye. "I'll tell you anything you want to know."

"When was your last date?"

"Four and a half years ago."

"And how have you kept yourself pleasured since that time?"

"You're assuming that relationship was sexual, if that's the question."

"Assuming it wasn't, how so?"

"I have a little pink friend at home, but mostly with my fingers."

"Show me."

One of the greatest secrets a woman holds deeply and extremely personal is sexually gratifying herself, and she will only engage in such a private act in a safe environment and only before someone she completely trusts not judgmental. It's an act the average man has never seen, even with his wife of many years.

"I never wear anything to bed," Ferrell said as she turned the cover back to expose her nudity. She placed her hand between her closed cream-colored thighs at first and began slowly stimulating her inner lips as she fixed her gaze on me. The more she moved her fingers, the wider she began spreading her legs apart, bringing them up so her feet were flat on the bed and her knees up to her breast, allowing me to see the pinkness of her inner lips as she spread them apart with two fingers, then one finger was inserted inside of her kitty. With the wetness of her finger, she came up to form a circular motion around her clitoris as her fingers moved up and down her vagina.

It wasn't long before I could see the vaginal lubrication seep from her core opening. Ferrell switched hands, her fingers moist, she ran her fingers over her lips as she fingered herself with her other hand in and out, up and down until she released an "ahh," as the rhythm of her fingers began to move rapidly and she swelled, and her lips became a deep flush red. I watched as she began to slide down the pillow, her legs spread wider, and fingers glossing as she pinpointed the spot that gave her the most pleasure and fingered that one spot for several minutes it seemed. Her mouth gaped open in jubilation and another, "Uhhh-humm," taking her tongue and licking her lips, toes curling upward as her back arched off the bed.

Not once did she take her eyes off me, her gaze was enticing my own nature to rise. She then inserted her finger deep inside her core, switched hands and wet her nipple with her own creme, it shined brightly and became erect, but she was in full thrust as she threw her head back and began vigorously pressing down and rocking her wet fingers over her g-spot as she reached, perhaps her second or third climax. With her head leaning back over the pillow, she came to a rest by locking eyes with me and down to my own rock-hard erection from watching her release.

I got up and walked out of the guest room, climbed in my own bed, giving her credit for opening up without hesitation.

I closed my eyes to the sounds of the shower running, thinking how a single act in life can set us apart from any other relationship we may encounter. That trust is the foundation of any relationship and any woman who holds a secret as natural as her desire to be fulfilled by her man or self-pleasure is a woman holding much deeper secrets about herself. Ferrell proved in action what she had put into words. Bottom line is if I was going to get personally involved with her risking my life defending her, then asking her for something of equal value that she held secret opened the door to limitless possibilities.

I must have had drifted off on the thought because when I opened my eyes again, Ferrell was standing in front of me, or at least I looked up at her fresh Brazilian waxed kitty.

"Is there anything else I must do to gain your trust?" she said unabashed.

I pulled the cover back on the other side of the bed and she climbed under them next to me.

"No one has ever asked me to do that before," she said.

"Good because I would have been disappointed to find out I wasn't your first."

"Did I disappoint you?"

"Not at all."

"Then why did you leave before I finished?"

"Because you gave me what I came for."

"Was that all you wanted?"

I did not respond.

"If you're going to ask me to do things like that, then I hope you wouldn't hold back from me."

I turned over to face her. "If we're going to trust our lives in each other's hands, then I have to know you trust me with everything you own and nothing less."

"So, was that my blood oath to you?"

"Far more than that."

"How so?"

"Because cum is thicker than blood."

"I just want you to know I wouldn't have done that for anyone else."

"So why did you do it for me?"

"Because I want to earn your trust."

"Tomorrow will be a busy day so we better get some sleep."

"Okay, but I have just one more question."

"What's that?"

"What would you have done if I had refused your request?"

"But you didn't."

"What if I had?" she said, sliding close enough for her body to touch mine.

"You would have had to find you way home," I said.

"I don't know if you missed the memo, but you're stuck with me and I hope that means I'm stuck with you," she said then nudged up against me tighter, as I squeezed my eyes tighter, having plenty of trouble keeping my erection on my side of the bed. Everything was swelling, my head, veins, and fluids were rushing through my body like a herd of buzzing bees to honeycomb. Her body forced her words into my mind

"I didn't say I was a virgin. No one has ever been in that bed with me or this house."

"Wow, so you're a hermit."

"This is where I come to get away from all the noise that no one knows I own."

"Oh, I see, your own private retreat."

"Yeah."

Ferrell was definitely an early bird, full of energy and very talkative.

"Are you always this serious 24/7?" she asked, pointing her fork at me after taking a mouth full of scrambled eggs. She giggled, "I mean, you even eat serious."

"I'm just sitting here eating."

Ferrell took a bite of my toast and began chewing it to emulate how she pictured me eating. We both then laughed at her poor attempt to copy me.

"See now that's much better," she said.

"But that's not what you were talking about a few minutes ago."

"No, I was thinking about how you were such a gentleman last night by not taking advantage of me. I admire your self-restraint in not giving in to your nature that wouldn't go down."

"You saw that?"

"Actually, I felt it pressing against me." She smirked.

"So, you liked the idea of tormenting me?"

"I'm just wondering how long you can resist."

"I just want to make sure I'm not filling a void and what we do between us is about us."

"What I did was only fair after what you made me do to establish our bond and then walked out on me."

"I didn't make you do anything."

"Yes, you did."

"I don't recall holding a gun to your head."

"But your words are more powerful than a gun."

"So, you're mad?"

"At first I was because I thought you were taking advantage of me, and you were hoping I refused so you would have an excuse to reject me. But I felt different after I climbed in your bed and you went sleep."

". . .And?"

"After you mentioned not wanting to fill a void and you wanted what happens between us to be about us, I got over being upset with you."

"Did I say all of that?"

"In less words, yes you did."

"Okay, this talk was good, as well as breakfast but we really need to get moving."

Ferrell got up and brushed toast crumbs from her pants. "Since you're already handsomely dressed, I hope you don't mind putting the dishes away while I finish getting dressed."

"I can handle it from here," I said, standing up and grabbing the dishes from the table.

"I won't be long," she said, brushing her breast pass me as if we were in a tight space passing each other.

I watched the form of her tanned body leave the room, thinking nothing that beautiful should ever bring the kind of trouble I was feeling in desiring her. This was a made woman; testing her loyalty was one thing but having intercourse with her would be mixing business with pleasure.

I scraped the plates clean and put them in the dishwasher with the pots, glasses, and silverware.

Money rubs shoulders with money just as like minds gravitates to like minds. Ferrell was like a breath of fresh air, in the sense that although she's now a major distributor expanding across state lines, not once had she mentioned it nor seemed flattered by the idea that the Queen of the South had nothing on her. This was unlike the pressure I faced with Medina, who constantly rode me about finding a different business to be in, I thought as I pulled the car out of the garage while Ferrell finished getting dressed.

"You're not going to lock the door?" Ferrell asked as she got in the passenger's seat and closed her door.

"It's a double lock," I said, dropping the car in reverse and backing out of the driveway.

"Can I ask where we're going?" She wanted to know as I pulled up to the corner stop sign.

"I'm taking you home."

That drew silence from her as I got on 696 Expressway. "Yeah," I said into my phone after dialing Castro's number. "Put your man on the phone, Nicky."

"Hold on a minute," she said, and yelling for Castro to pick up the phone.

"I got it," he yelled. "Hello."

"What's the news?" I asked.

"Nothing, this Covid shit got these kids driving me crazy," he said, sounding agitated.

I was passing the street he lived on after coming up off the expressway.

"You haven't been watching the news?" he inquired. "Muthfuckah's dropping like flies by the second and this crazy ass President-Trump's done, got banned from Twitter."

"Naw, you watch enough news for the both of us."

"Yeah, while you're running around like this virus ain't killing people all over the world," he said. "And I bet you're not even wearing the Spooky mask I gave you."

Hardly anyone was wearing mask after the country came off lockdown. I noticed Ferrell didn't wear one either.

"Yeah, I got them right here with me," I said, but the mask he gave with a pair of broken cuffs on them were in the glove compartment where they had been ever since he gave them to me, unless I went somewhere they were required. "But what's going on with our news?"

"Same thing, we paid Rakehell a visit and they were ready to go the distance until we torched their safe house. Now they're on the run."

"And that was on the news?" I asked, pulling in front of the Valentino mansion, and before I could stop Ferrell had already pushed the remote control and the gate was opening.

"No, that wasn't on the news, but their club was until the fire department got the flames under control."

I pulled up to the front door and noticed the gate closing from my rearview mirror.

"Alright, I'll catch up with you later," I said, about to hang up.

"Lion, wait!"

"I'm here."

"We tapped into Rakehell's line, and you might want to check in on Pharaoh."

"What's up with Pharaoh?"

"That shit, Earthquake's moving faster than he thought it would."

"Okay, let's slide through there as well. You got a Rakehell to turn?"

"Something like that."

"Where you holding him?"

"Crazy-Eight's stash house."

"Meet me there."

"On my way, one."

"One," I said, and hung up.

"Something wrong?" I asked Ferrell.

"You're not coming in?" she asked without looking at me.

"I can't."

She opened her door and started to get out, then leaned back in her seat and closed the door. "It won't take me long to change clothes or I can just grab some of my things real fast."

"Sooner or later, you have to go in there."

"We can come back and have dinner together after you're done," she said. "I mean, we're in this together so I don't know why I can't go with you if it's business you're taking care of.". . . I started the engine.

"Good," Ferrell almost leaped in my lap and kissed me. Aside from being talkative in the mornings, she was very affectionate. "You're going to have to get used to this, you know?" she said, her bubbly spirit returned to her personality.

"Get used to what, you kissing me?" I said, backing out of the driveway as the gate reopened.

"That, too," she said.

"What's the other?"

"Getting used to the fact that not only am I your co-pilot for a while but I'm also your First Lady, so we're inseparable."

That I could not contest, no matter how much I wanted to renounce the latter. And because of the fact she had every right to participate in the family business, I could not contest the former either.

"I can't come in; you can just jump fresh while I make a few calls and we have to get moving."

Before I could complete my sentence, Ferrell was out of the door and bouncing up the steps heading into the house.

Chapter
11

TWENTY MINUTES LATER, JUST AS FERRELL HAD BOUNCED UP THE STAIRS, she was just as full of zest dashing out the door and back down the steps, her black hair floating on the air.

"That didn't take long, did it?" she asked, closing her door and putting on her seatbelt all in one motion.

She stopped and looked at me. "I'm sorry, did I take too long?"

"No, you weren't long."

"Oh, I have to learn your expressions."

She looked at me and I head gestured back towards the gate for her to open it.

"Why didn't you say something?" She laughed and grabbed my forearm, followed by pulling the gate opener out and pushing the button.

The changed outfit was an interesting choice — burgundy slacks, and black blouse with matching shoes. The same color as the Cadillac we had changed into. It was burgundy with a black interior.

"I'm going to have to start carrying a gun if you're going to be dressing like that," I said, backing out of the driveway and heading straight for I-75 Freeway back into the city.

"Is it too much?" Ferrell asked. "See, that's why you should have come inside with me while I changed."

"Out here it's casual, but we're going where the boys in the hood where designer clothes draw less attention than a quality look."

"Well, I didn't wear it for the boys in the hood," she smiled. "Maybe you can take me shopping for some more suitable wear."

"Only problem with that is I don't think anything you wear could diminish your attractiveness."

Ferrell blushed. "I feel safe with you wearing absolutely nothing."

I think I blushed. . ."Well, you better because I don't think you've ever hung out on the westside of Detroit."

"Is it that bad?"

"You wanted to come so you'll be able to judge for yourself in a few minutes."

"Now you're scaring me, Lion," she said, as we came up off the Lodge Freeway onto Clairmount Street and took it down to 12th Street and Rosa Park Boulevard, down to Gladstone where I parked out front.

"This won't take long," I said, turning the engine off.

"Andrew mentioned this street before," Ferrell looked up

and studied the house. "Is this where you came to last night that had you so upset?"

"This is where Pharaoh lives."

"I can't go in there, Lion."

"Then I'll be back in a few minutes."

I knew that I'd be longer than a few minutes because Castro's car was nowhere in sight, which meant I was early.

"Wait a minute, you can't leave me out here alone like this."

"You're not alone," I said. "Do you see the blue Dodge on the opposite side of the road with the guy in it?"

She squinted as if she needed glasses. "Yes."

"He'll be watching this car, so you'll be safe."

"Who is he?" she asked in an untrusting tone.

"He's employed by the family."

"No, Lion."

"What do you mean, no?"

"I don't know, this just doesn't feel right."

"It's a dope house filled with drugs and where people come to shoot smack in their veins. It's not supposed to feel right unless you're a junkie looking for a fix."

"But…""There is no but," I said. "Listen to me, if we're going to work as a team together, you're going to have to trust my moves and when I move, you got to step with me as if they're your moves by nature. I tried to spare you from this disease by dropping you off at your home, but you insisted on being my wingman. The seed has been planted and the shit that's in the fertilizer is a part of the seeds' growth and once you step in this shit, there's no getting the scent out your brain. This is all a part of what we have to deal with to survive."

This was no pep talk to get Ferrell's head in winning a basketball or volleyball tournament, but a game of life that produced people like Pharaoh and his junkie friends. There was no shallow way to introduce her into the game other than to throw her into the deep end where shark eats guppies. This was dirty work that often got bloody.

"I just didn't imagine it would be –"

"This real?" I interjected

"This is all coming so fast."

I could not restrain my laugh.

"It's not funny Lion, please don't do that."

"You're right, it isn't, and I shouldn't be laughing," I said. "Look, these are people just like us, no different. They just suffer from their addictions. We serve social workers, bus drivers, police, cooks, and people you wouldn't imagine are hooked on drugs. Some of these people help keep this city running and clean."

"I never thought about it that way."

Pharaoh did not actually push any of the kinds of drugs ran by the Legion family. Earthquake was my product that I made as a sideline investment. But if what Ferrell had told me was true about Andrew tailing my private activities, then she'd know Pharaoh was being supplied by me.

"We're here now, and I'm not leaving without taking care of this business, so you can either come inside with me or sit here until I'm done," I said in a definite tone. "Now the choice is yours."

I got out of the car, walked around the front, and stood there to allow Ferrell time to process her options, until she opened her door and got out of the car.

Ferrell had every right to be sensitive about going into a drug house around people she knew nothing about where needles were being injected recreationally. If Pharaoh wasn't family, I would not have ever seen a needle being pushed into the veins by anyone that was not wearing a nurse's or doctors' uniform in a hospital myself.

Chapter
12

PHARAOH OPENED THE FRONT DOOR, UNLOCKED THE burglar bars in a panic, and left the keys dangling in the lock, spun around, and dashed up the hall at lightning speed.

"Lock the door Lion, I'll be with you in a minute!" He was yelling through the house.

There was a lot of commotion coming from the back of the house. "Ant, stay with us!" was yelled.

Ferrell stepped inside, and I looked up the main street to see if Castro was in sight before stepping inside and locking the door behind me. Ferrell was so close to me I could hardy turn around without bumping into her. She was frozen in her tracks and listening to the numerous calls for Ant to stay awake.

"What's going on?" she asked, eyes stretched wide.

"Come on," I said, escorting her into the living room. "Have a seat, I'll be right back."

"Get some ice, young blood!" Old man Hawkins barked an

order to me as if we were in the military and he was my drill instructor.

They were frantically trying to save their friend's life from overdosing. I didn't move from my position where I stood watching them drag Ant's limp body up and down the narrow hallway, barely capable of walking side by side. They were almost walking sideways up the hall.

Pharaoh was sweating up a storm with a gray drying towel wrapped around his neck. Between his yelling and old man Hawkins being a drill sergeant over death, you would have thought it was ten people in a verbal scuffle.

"If he overdosed," I said, "take his ass down the alley and dump him in a vacant house."

For a brief second, my instructions restored calm.

"Got damn man!" Pharaoh yelled. "Keep him moving!."

"That's some cold shit to say, young blood," Hawkins exclaimed.

"I'm not about to spend a single hour being questioned by homicide and trying to explain what I was doing while a junkie was shooting up dope in this house," I said. "Now if you can't save him, 911 will not be called to this house."

One look at Pharaoh, and his silence for the first time since I had walked through the door sobered him up enough to understand what I was saying to be true.

They kept that up until Ant was no longer dragging his feet on the floor and was semiconscious, at which point they began pumping his stomach with wild Irish Rose cheap wine as he staggered from the grips of death, and I returned to the living room to join Ferrell, sitting down next to her on the sofa.

⟨✺⟩

"Is everything okay?" she asked out of curiosity.

"Yeah, it's all good," I responded.

"I know this may be a bad time but I have to use the bathroom."

"Straight to the back and off to the left, the door is open."

Ferrell got up, went to the bathroom and was back so fast and even more shaken than she was before going to the back.

"Oh my god!" she said in a panic voice. "I'm sorry, the door wasn't open, so I knocked on it and no one answered so I opened it and I think there's a dead man in there!"

"What the fuck!?" I jumped up thinking they had let Ant kill over. "This is why I didn't want to be bothered with this shit."

"I'm sorry," Ferrell said, glued so close to me she had stepped on the heels of my shoe twice

Ferrell had left the door partly open, so I swung it open to witness a bloody mess. It was another one of Pharaoh's white customer-friends, nodding off on the toilet with a spike needle injected into his groin with his penis laying limp to the side, the syringe laid on the floor next to his pant down to his ankles. He left the needle in his groin while trying to refill the syringe with the rest of the drugs but nodded off and the cotton ball came out of the needle, causing blood to skeet all over the place.

"Is he dead?" Ferrell asked."Yo!" I yelled, while slapping on the door with an open hand. "Yo!"He lifted his head in slow motion, then jerking out of a nod. "Jees-us!" he slurred. "I'm sorry, bro."

"Pull your pants up and clean this shit up!" I didn't wait for a response before closing him inside the bloody mess he'd made. The others, I noticed had went into the basement to continue getting high.

"There's another bathroom upstairs," I said to Ferrell, leading the way upstairs.

"You okay?" I asked, looking back down at her as we reached the top landing of the stairs.

"I don't know, yeah I guess," she said, "but I'm going to pee myself if someone else is in here like that."

Reality for some people takes some time getting used to especially when they've been sheltered all of their lives from the evils of the world.

The bathroom was clean and empty.

"None of this bothers you?" she whispered.

"No one gets used to seeing that shit, you just grow numb to what you can and grow thick skin to the rest."

"Will you stand by the door until I'm done, please?" she asked, holding onto the doorknob.

"I'll be right here," I assured her.

I stood guard while Ferrell relieved herself and opened the door looking like she had flushed all of her stress down the toilet.

"There," she said, "I don't think I could have held that another second.

"Who are you?" I asked, looking over her shoulder.

She turned and looked at me puzzled.

"You're not the nervous woman I just escorted in there."

She laughed. "Oh my god Lion," she moved closer and touched my arm, "I thought you were serious for a moment."

"You tight?"

"Yes, I'm tight."

"Come here, I want to show you something." I closed the space between us, backing her into the bathroom, closed the door and kissed her lips gently, sucking on her lips and French kissing her with my tongue sliding in her mouth until she closed her eyes. That lasted eons in my mind but was more like a few minutes.

"That was surprisingly unexpected," she said, arms wrapped around my neck.

"Now look into the mirror," I said, stepping behind her and pressing my kahuna firmly against her love deluxe as I wrapped my arms around her waist.

"Lion not here," her cheeks turned blush.

"That would not be very romantic, I know. Look at yourself in the mirror," I pointed out. "I want you to keep this moment in your mind whenever we're out on business and never show any signs of shock or fear. The people you are going to encounter look for weakness to exploit. If you give them an inch, they'll take a mile, and since you're with me, they will come at me by trying to come through you."

She turned around still in my arms. "Is this what Andrew was talking about when he said seeing us together was almost scary?" Then kissed me before I could answer.

I looked over her shoulder, back into her eyes and said, "The wise don't get old by being fools, and sometimes we have to have blind faith in their knowledge."

"I think you may be right."

"I should be your only weakness and your greatest source of strength. Allowing the rest of the world to see only your power. So, let's see what you got behind those beautiful eyes."

Ferrell lead the way back downstairs without hesitation. I was still curious as to why Mr. Valentino made the wise decision to matchmake Ferrell and me. He knew more about her and me while we were discovering each other by the second. One thing I was sure of is that she didn't have to be told twice what to do and what should never be repeated. She exhibited all of the hallmarks of a lioness in her ability to adapt to changes as they developed."

Well hello there," Pharaoh greeted Ferrell no sooner than we stepped back into the living room as if it was his first time seeing her standing next to me.

"Hello, Mr. Pharaoh," she returned the gesture, hand held out as she moved away from my side, "I'm Ferrell Valentino."

They shook hands. "Pleased to meet you, Miss Valentino."

"Ferrell, just call me Ferrell."

Pharaoh presented a smile as bright as a sixty-watt light bulb. "Please have a seat."

"Thank you," she said, sitting in the same seat she had taken earlier that was across from Pharaoh.

"So, where you find my nephew at Ferrell?"

"Beverly Hills."

"When were you in California?"

"Oh no. Beverly Hills, Michigan," she corrected him.

"You been hiding her from me, huh?"

"We're out on business, she's a business associate," I said. "This is all nice, but we're going to have to save the small talk for another time. Right now, my main concern is what's going on with Earthquake and its marketability."

"Boyyy," Pharaoh started with a cracked smile. "We might have to hire some help the way Earthquake is selling.

"So it doesn't need to be cut?"

"No, it's the best in the city."

"If it's that good, we may have to shut down your shoot-up gallery after what I've seen here today. The family would come down hard on me if something happened to you."

"You worry too much, Lion," he said, standing up once he saw me and Ferrell stand to leave.

"Well, it's my ass not yours."

"I'll slow it down," he said. "Nice to meet you Ferrell."

"Take care, Pharaoh."

Talking about cutting the dope was the last thing he wanted to hear and rushed us out of the door.

Chapter 13

CASTRO WAS WAITING BESIDE MY CAR WHEN FERRELL and I stepped onto the front porch. The look on his face was what you might see of shock and awe of a beautiful woman.

"This is the Lion family's first lieutenant, Castro," I said to her as we descended the stairs. "What's up my man? This is the Legion family's First Lady, Ferrell Valentino, the new Capo."

"Hello Castro," she interjected. "You can call me Ferrell."

"At your service, Miss Ferrell." He shook her hand and looked down at her ring.

"You're the one I talked to yesterday before putting Andrew on the phone."

"Andrew?" Castro looked confused.

"Yes, Mr. Valentino."

"Oh snap, the old man, that was you?"

Ferrell took her hand back and smiled. "Yes, that was me."

I opened the passenger's side to let Ferrell in. "I need to speak to Castro in private and we'll be on our way."

"Oh, okay," she said. "It was nice to meet you Castro."

"Likewise," he shook her hand again.

"This won't take long," I told her before closing her door and handing her the keys. "You can start the car to get some heat in there."

We walked to the front of the car. "I be damned, she's the boss-of-bosses of the Legion family?"

"That's her," I said.

"Holy sweet mother Jesus!" He looked at Ferrell then back at me. "Was that why the old man wanted to see you?"

"Yeah."

"Man, this some real twenty first century shit," he said, "and she's fine as fuck!"

"That's not all."

"That's not all, what's bigger than a woman becoming a Don?" he chuckled. "I didn't know if I should shake her hand or kiss her ring."

"The old man gave me his ring before he retired to Florida."

Castro looked like I had just grown a third eye. "Impossible. You got to be bullshittin' me, man."

"Got it back at the house."

"What does this mean, you got Legion juice now too?"

"We're fifty/fifty on both sides of the table."

"Kiss my black ass," he said. "Congratulations, man, on some real shit!"

"Not just yet my friend."

"Now what the fuck does that supposed to mean?" Castro frowned. "You didn't turn him down, did you?"

"No, I couldn't. That's why she's with me."

His smiled returned. "Damn, and you're on a first name basis with her, she must like you."

"I've been introducing her to the other families, or that's my plan for the week."

"Was that why I couldn't reach you last night? Oh hell no, did you fuck her!?" "Okay, what's up with the Rakehell business?" I said, dodging the question.

"Fuck them, did you fuck her? That's what I want to know."

"I'm going need you to focus right now, man."

"Steve called the Crazy-Eight and they went to pick him up. He's over there being interrogated but the muthfuckah won't say shit cause he knows they can't kill him with all he knows."

"Let's go over there and see if we can loosen up his tongue," I said, walking around to the driver's side of the car.

"Meet you there," Castro said, eyeing Ferrell once more before heading towards his car.

He waited until I turned around before pulling off, taking lead in front of me as I followed behind him.

ᏬᏬᏬ

He did not take the expressway as I thought he would, but took the main streets down Clairmount to Linwood Street, made a right turn and proceeded down Linwood until we passed one of the Rakehell's clubs near Tyler Street. The club was burnt to a crisp, which I assumed is what he wanted me to see. Ferrell was silent as she studied the inner-city neighborhood until her phone went off.

She smiled, grabbing her purse saying, "Is that yours or mine?"

Before I could respond the ringing got louder as she pulled her phone out.

"Hi, how was your flight?" she said. "No way, shut up."

By the time we reached the light on Division, Ferrell's gleefulness turned serious. "Yes, we're together," she touched my hand. "He's taking good care of me, Andrew. I haven't left his side since we left the house." The conversation went on with a bunch of, "Yes of course," and "it'll be fine," as we drove across the city.

"Lion speaking," I said into my own phone after receiving a call.

It was a call from one of the guys at the interrogation house. "Why are you calling me, Castro is taking point on this."

"I did, he's not picking up," Blast said in my ear. "The Rakehells know we have one of their men and I think they're trying to shut him up before we get him talking. They just shot the place to hell."

I took a deep breath as Ferrell looked over at me and was pointing at her phone. I nodded an 'okay' to her.

"Did they make it out?" I asked Blast, as I switched lanes to catch up to Castro, and pulled beside him at the red light, lowered the window, waving my phone out to him.

"My shit died on me," he said.

"Mr. Valentino," I said into Ferrell's phone as I was handing her my phone. "How's the weather down there?" I asked.

Ferrell took my phone and handed it out the window to Castro just as the light turned green.

"Great, it's beautiful down here," he said.

"That's great," I said tailing Castro.

"Ferrell has had nothing but good things to say about you," he said. "I knew you were the one to pair her with."

"I can't see how because all she's been seeing is the dirty side of the business so far."

"I need you to get her safely to the next destination, she'll tell you the details."

"Consider it done, Mr. Valentino," I said looking over at her.

"Good," he said. "Give us what we want Lion, our blood is rich. Now put Ferrell back on the phone."

"He wants to talk back to you," I held the phone out to her.

"You didn't tell him, did you Andrew?" Ferrell looked at me for a sign.

Castro was pushing near ninety up a side street according to my gauge, and zig zagging in and out of traffic on the main streets.

"I love you too Andrew, bye." She ended the phone call taking a deep breath. "Are you taking me home?" she asked.

"First, I need to know what Andrew was talking about saying you'll explain what it is to me," I said, still watching my speed gauge as I stayed close to Castro's bumper.

"They want to meet with me."

"Whose they"?

"The old table."

"You lost me."

Ferrell did not seem too thrilled about filling me in on her conversation with Andrew.

"You have to take me home," she said nervously.

"Right now?"

"Yes, right now," she insisted. "Andrew has set everything in motion."

"Wait, wait," I said, then realized I was slowing down or Castro was picking up speed. "You just got off the phone with him."

"I have to be on the next flight to Gran Paradiso."

"Where's that located?"

"Italy. They want to meet me. I have to go, or it would be a show of disrespect if I didn't."

This was all new to me, being bossed around by old men with power from another country, and it's no wonder the mob can't be touched, you can't destroy what you can't reach. And when you're in the company of people who can put you on a plane just because someone wants to look you in the face, that's the kind of power many men would kill for, and I was escorting the First Lady wielding that same power to be the one being sent for. My power was a neighborhood thing that stretched up a few miles and up an alley, while these people ran olive fields that was secluded away from prying eyes and that shit excited the hell out of me just knowing I was in the grip of such power. Who wants to be president from four to eight years when you can be untouchable for life? I thought about the ring given to me and my reluctance to put it on.

"What time does your flight leave?" I asked.

"As soon as I get to the airport."

I just smiled, thinking that this woman had not left my side in the past twenty-four hours and not once had she used her phone, at least not in my presence, yet with one phone call she was about to hop on a private flight out of the country.

"Can I see your phone?" I asked.

I dialed Castro. "Yeah, change of plans," I said.

He pulled over on the service drive and yelled.

"I'll hit you up later," I said, "I got to handle something else."

"Hit me up when you're done," he said.

"Alright, keep me in the loop."

"Later," he said. "Stay safe."

We both got back on the road heading in different directions.

"You don't seem too thrilled to be going to your homeland," I said.

"No it's not that," she began, as I begin to get near her home. "It's just everything is happening so fast and—" she paused and looked over at me, "I don't know how to say it."

"As long as what you want to say is what you feel inside, then say what you feel," I said to help her find the words.

"We were just starting to make a connection and now I have to leave."

"When you get back, we'll talk about the idea of moving closer. This trip isn't moving us apart, it's actually going to bring us closer."

"Did Andrew talk to you about us living together?

"And the B-word?"

"You say that like it's a bad thing."

"Oh my god, I'm going to kill him."

"Seems like this family has things planned for the both of us."

"Don't think of it that way," she said. "This will be our decision so don't let Andrew pressure you into doing anything you're not ready for."

"I've been doing this for a while now, you're like the best part of a long journey home."

"In that case," Ferrell smiled and held out the remote control, "this will be yours, and you have to promise me you'll water the plants while I'm gone."

I took the remote and opened the gates, and pulled up to the front door.

"Come on, you have to help me pick out what to wear."

I got out of the car, pushed the remote to close the gate and followed Ferrell into the house.

All honeymoons began with high hopes for the future. But a marriage made by the bosses of the underworld was like going on a vacation on an exotic unexplored island, especially where mixing blood was involved. If any side were to disagree with the arrangement, a honeymoon could turn into a tsunami. Was that why Ferrell's family were sending for her, or could it be she was going to receive their blessing? That remained to be seen, either way I would be waiting for her to return with whatever the news would be.

Chapter 14

FERRELL'S BEDROOM WAS ON THE BACKSIDE OF THE mansion on the second floor and the drawn drapes that led to the balcony showed the landscape of the entire golf course and the other far-off mansions on the other side of the illustrious landscape. Her bedroom was twice the size of any bedroom I had ever been in. It was divided into an entertainment sectional on one side of the room and held a queen size near the picture window. Next to the windows were a plush soft leather rocker recliner that let out into a lazy boy that was angled to allow the view outside as well as full sight of the opposite end of the room where Ferrell was moving around packing.

She had been out of sight most of the time and mostly dashing from the dresser to the closet and laying clothes out on the bed. I watched and was beginning to wonder how she was going to get all of the clothes in the few suitcases she had laid out.

"Which one should I wear?" she asked, stepping out of the walk-in closet wearing a red skirt, one red pump heel and a thin lace brassiere she held up and two blouses on hangers, pressing one after the other over the skirt for a match.

"The black one," I pointed out, studying her delicate frame and oval hips.

"But do you like what you see?" She struck pose and twisted her hip towards me.

"I would show you how much I do if you didn't have a plane to catch."

Ferrell grabbed her chest and gazed at me speechless, then hopped back inside the closet. I heard her clear her throat before saying, "You can't just sit there Lion, help me!" She yelled from the closet, "I don't know how to dress for these things, and I trust your judgment."

"I'm right here," I said standing behind her.

"Wooh!" she laughed. "Damn Lion, you scared me."

I just smiled. I was not intending to scare her but she was bent over when I walked into the closet and I did not want to disrupt the motion of her ass twisting to get into a different outfit.

"What do you want me to do?"

"Here button me up."

The black blouse buttoned from the back.

"Why did you pick this one, I won't be with you to unbutton it."

She twisted back to look back at me. "I'm going to miss this. You, I'm going to miss you. Is that crazy seeing that we've only been around each other for two days?"

"Hopefully you won't be gone long enough to miss me. Besides, this will be good for us."

"How so?"

"It will give us time to contemplate what we're feeling and to see if it fades or intensify because of the distance." I finished buttoning Ferrell's blouse and she turned around to face me. I took her in my arms. "Are you wearing one shoe to the airport?"

She looked down at her feet and laughed. "No silly, I was just seeing if you liked this one best."

Every part of my body began to rise. "If I don't let go of you, you're going have a hard time explaining to the family why you missed your flight."

"Oh shit!" She bounced around trying to get into the other shoe. "Can you call and give them the time we will be arriving?"

"Okay, what airline are you taking?" I asked, walking out of the closet, "so I can see how much time we have to get you there."

Ferrell followed behind me as she was folding clothes and packing them into the suitcases on the bed. "It's a private plane, Skybridge. The number is in my roller decks next to the phone on my nightstand."

"Damn," I said, pushing one of the suitcases to the middle of the bed to make room for me to sit down, where I started thumbing through the roller decks until I saw Skybridge and its number.

"Hello, this is Tod your Skybridge customer service helpline, how may I help you?"

"Yeah," I said, "I'm calling to confirm the schedule for Ms. Ferrell Valentino."

"I apologize Mr. Valentino, I did not know it was you." Tod

began scrambling around. "Yes, as soon as you can give us your ETA, it should take no less than half an hour for takeoff."

I started to correct Tod, by telling him I was not Mr. Valentino, but the way Ferrell was looking at me and her joyous spunk, what did it matter? Besides, I was dragging Ferrell into my world showing her all its chaos, while she stood there silently showing me her world and all its influence.

"Thank you," I said to Tod. "We'll be arriving within the hour."

"Very well Mr. Valentino, I'll notify your pilot at once."

"Is everything okay?" Ferrell asked.

"Everything's fine. All I have to do is get you there."

"Good, now come help me zip this closed."

"Do you need all of this?" I asked as we both leaned on the suitcase and zipped it close.

"Lion, a woman can never have too many clothes."

I began loading everything in the trunk while Ferrell ran around making sure she didn't forget anything. She finally came out of the house and jumped into the car, and I closed her door.

"I hope I didn't forget anything," she said as I started the car, opened the gate, and pulled onto the street. As soon as the gate was pulling close, I pulled off heading for the airport.

"Can I see your watch?" Ferrell asked.

I extended my wrist so she could see the time.

"No, give it to me," she said, grabbing my arm and began taking off my watch.

"The clock right there is correct."

"I can't take it with me."

I got on the expressway minus a watch. "This is nice," she said. "How many of these do you have?"

"Only one of that kind."

"Do you wear this one often?"

"Yeah, I do."

"So you'll miss it if I keep it?"

I just smiled.

"Then it's settled."

"What's settled?"

"Now that I know you'll miss it, you'll have to think of me every time you look for the time."

"What if I said you can't take it?"

"Too late, I already have it," she said. "You should have said you were going to miss me and then I wouldn't have to take it."

"I am going to miss you."

She laughed. "No, that's not how it works. It's too late now. So, what of mine do you want?"

"To see your body getting off your plane."

She looked at me and blushed. "I do too, but you have to keep something personal to me."

"Okay," I said, looking over at her and back on the road, "but this may hurt a bit."

Ferrell's mouth fell open as if in shock by my words.

"Well?" she said impatiently.

"What's in your purse?"

"Well, let's see." She began taking one item out at a time. "I'm almost out of goodies."

"That's it," I said.

"These, why would you want nail clippers?"

I came up off the expressway heading straight for the airport.

"Because I don't want you to bite you nails off," I said.

"Why would I do that?"

"Just the baby pinky," I said, handing her the clippers. "Cut it off and give it to me."

"Are you serious?" Ferrell asked. "I can't cut my fingernail off, Lion," she said, looking at them.

I pulled into the airport's parking lot with Ferrell still looking down at her nails.

"Can you choose something else to take?" she pleaded.

"Every time you look down at your missing finger nail it will remind you that a part of you has been cut off."

"That's not fair," she pouted a sad face, then cut off the French cotton candy colored nail.

I took it from her hand. "Before this fingernail grows back, I want you back on that plane heading back to me."

Ferrell accepted her loss with a deep breath. "You can be a real asshole, you know? And have an unconventional way of testing loyalty."

"Come on, let's get you out of here," I grabbed the door handle. "Wait, you're not wearing a mask?"

"Oh darn it, I knew I was forgetting something."

"Here," I opened the glove compartment, "take these."

"Who's Spooky?" she asked, looking at the mask.

"Something Castro's into and gave me."

She put the mask on and looked into the mirror. "It's different, and you better have my fingernail when I get back because if you don't, I won't forgive you."

"What?" I asked.

"I'm not playing," she said, pulling the mask from her mouth, down to her chin.

ↃↀↃↀↃ

"Leave them," Ferrell said as I was pulling her luggage from the trunk. "The handlers will come for them. I wish you were coming with me."

"Sounds like a real break that would do me good."

"It's a private flight and I'll be flying alone so if you want to come with me, it'll be fun."

I strongly considered the idea for a second. "I have to stay and clean things up here or the families will tear each other apart," I said, opening the door and she stepped inside the airport.

"I guess you're right."

"Besides that, they might kill my Black ass if I showed up in Italy with you snuggled up in my arms."

"Oh don't say that, Lion," Ferrell said as we approached the airlines desk. "And just in case you forgot," she held up her pinky finger, Valentino ring, "I have juice over there. If anyone was to harm a single hair on your beautiful head, I would go to war for you."

I don't know if the flight attendant overheard Ferrell's declaration but by the look on her face and if I was a gambling man, I'd say she had.

"Hi, I'm Ms. Valentino, I have a departure on Skybridge." "Yes

89

Ms. Valentino," the woman's face lit up as she jumped to serve Ferrell. "Robin, will you take over the desk, thank you," she said. "Your luggage, where's your luggage?" she asked in a rush as if she was about to grab it personally.

"They're in the burgundy Cadillac."

"Oh okay," she said, "excuse me for a moment. Ray, I need a luggage pickup."

"Where is it?" Ray asked.

"It's the burgundy Cadillac DTS," I said, handing him the keys.

"This way please, Ms. Valentino."

I could hear the plane engine running rapidly.

"That's kind of small to be flying overseas, isn't it?"

Ferrell giggled, "That's the plane taking me to Skybridge."

"Looks like this is where we part ways."

"Which I thought I wasn't good at."

"I've never put anyone on a plane before," was my excuse.

"Do I get a hug?"

I put my arms around Ferrell and we kissed for a long time until the flight attendant cleared her windpipes.

"You better get going before I start crying."

"I didn't see you like this when Andrew left."

"He's my brother, the emotions are different."

"I'll be here to pick you up when you get back."

I stood there watching Ferrell rush towards the attendant and the two of them disappeared through the exit door heading for her plane.

The luggage handler carted Ferrell's suitcases up to me.

"Your keys, Mr. Valentino," and sped off in one swooping motion as he rushed to make sure Ferrell's luggage left with her.

The human connection can only be measured by parting ways. When the sun goes down and the flowers fold in on itself yearning to be comforted by the sun's warmth once again.

Chapter 15

AFTER KEEPING MY WORD WITH MR. VALENTINO AND handling the Legion family business, it was time to get in the mud and dish out some Lion family justice to the Rakehell family.

I had to come up off the freeway to make a call when I realized I didn't get my phone back from Castro, I pulled up to L. Georges Coney Island to use their phone to call Castro.

"Hello," Castro answered his phone on the third ring.

"Where you at?" I asked.

"We're in the basement," he said.

"I'm on my way."

"It's bloody down here, you still got the Valentino First Lady with you?"

"I dropped her off," I said. "Why you ask?"

"Because she's been blowing up your phone."

"Say, what she wanted?" "Man, I'm not your love connection," Castro said jokingly. "What the fuck did you do to her?" I laughed. "I'm on my way," I said and hung up the phone. Ferrell was in the air trying to reach back to me before her plane could land. The thought of her calling brought a smile to my face as I slid back in the driver's seat. If only my life was as smooth as pulling out of the parking lot with the lights turning green upon my approach, but it was more of a dirty grayish slush like the street I rode on. I thought about if it was possible to keep Ferrell off these streets, but eventually some dirt is going to rub off when you're playing in mud.

The basement was another interrogation sight of the Crazy-Eight where most men or women that went there never saw their next near kin. Its location was undisclosed and for that reason, if you weren't blindfolded going in, you could be assured you weren't coming from the basement standing on the feet that brought you down there.

"What's up, Lion?" Blast asked, answering the door and closing it once I stepped inside the smelly house that held the stench of stale blood, pine soil, and bleach.

"Wassup," I responded to Blast.

"Man, these boys have been hovering over dude like hungry vultures," he said, following behind me as I walked down the basement staircase and came upon a military tent and a drop cloth floor covering.

"You eight's had any sleep in the past forty eight hours?" I asked, looking over at the Rakehell who was strapped down to a makeshift execution table.

"My man," I said to the Rakehell who looked like he'd been put through hell, "you got something for me?"

"I don't know anymore," the battered man exclaimed. "I came to you with valuable information and, this," he lifted up his hands from the scraps, "is how your men treat me!?""Give me something my men can go out and confirm, and there may be a saving grace for you, a fate I can assure you your family won't be offered," I said, moving to stand over him.

"Bullshit!! Cut me lose and then we can talk. I done shitted on myself and these mutherfuckers getting their rocks off torturing me."

The Crazy-Eight's sense of humor was alive if nothing else and they got a good chuckle out of Rakehell's ranting.

"No, here's the deal muthafuckah," I said. "You're going to give me a reason to dismiss them to check out your lead, and when they come back and tell me you haven't wasted my time, then I'll consider giving you something in return. Because if you've had me drop what I was doing to play some game with you, they'll take you apart limb by limb until shitting on yourself will be the last best memory you'll enjoy."

"The big bad Lion has spoken," he said. "You think I don't know how this shit is going to happen, why do you think I came to you? I'd say by now you have half the city tracking us down and you won't stop until we're all dead. You don't need me for that, but what you will need me for is finding that bitch who started a war she can't finish."

I turned to walk away, "Cut him open until you find a part of him that likes to talk."

"Meyers and Grand River!" he yelled. "Last house off the corner with the red fence around it," Rakehell said to stop the assault and me from leaving. "Send your eight cubs over there and they'll get all the action they can handle."

Castro walked through the tent with the Tokyo Twins accompanying him.

"He finally got something to say, huh?" Castro said.

"I'm riding shotgun," Blast announced.

The Crazy-Eight left locked and loaded for action.

"Hey Blast," Ninon spoke as he passed her.

"What's good?" He said in passing.

"Where's Madame Cordelia, you stinky parasite?" Ninon asked, as cold as ice.

He laughed. "Bitch, why don't you suck my dick and share it with your sister."

"Lion, he's going to need to take some manners with him to the afterglow," Ninon said, seeking approval.

I walked over to one of the chairs that had just been abandoned by Blast, and sat down for the show.

"I like it rough you fine bitch."

I opened the palm of my hands, "Man's sexual fetish is calling out for stimulation."

This guy started out a freak for pain which quickly turned unpleasant for him as things were being done to him that would cause any man to change his attitude towards women.

"I think he's had enough ladies," I said, and got no lip service from Rakehell.

"We're going to sit here while you answer Lion's questions and when he's tired of your shit, we got some more torment for your Black ass!" Nin said.

"Wait, wait, wait!" Castro said, while coming to hand me my phone. "Sounds like Rakehell gave us a lead."

He coughed up a mouth full of blood, then laughed.

"What do you need?" I asked into the phone.

"They dug in," Blast yelled. "The eight's want to clean house."

"Wipe it clean," I said.

"We're clear to level the bitch!"

Those were the last words I heard from Blast.

"Now it's your turn," Rakehell said.

"Let him down and let him clean himself up," I instructed.

"I'm gonna let you down, but if you try anything it'll be your last," Nin said.

"See if we can find him some clean clothes upstairs."

"Who's the bitch now, bitch!" Nin said taking the scraps off the Rakehell. "This is new." She showed him a Chrome 44 Magnum. "I brought it the very first day I met your boss because I knew she was going to rub me the wrong way," she said, taking a step back as the Rakehellwas let loose.

"These will have to do," Castro returned with fresh clothes and handed them to our guest.

"Where can I change?" he asked.

"Right here," Nin taunted him. "Let us see how dirty your pistol is."

"Wait a minute!" Castro protested. "This ain't a strip club I don't want to see that."

Both the Tokyo Twins laughed, while Castro took the limping man to the other side of the basement where there was a shower and toilet.

The Rakehell known as Caveman, returned to the tent looking battered, bruised but clean.

"Have a seat," I told him.

He sat down gingerly.

"Why did you come to me and what deal are you looking to barter?"

"I just want out."

"What does that mean?"

"I got family in Indiana."

"Where's Madame Cordelia?"

"You're going to need more than your toy soldiers to reach her, but how do I know once I tell you won't kill me?" he said.

"I'm going to assume at best guess with your safehouse being hit, if I let you walk out of here right now, your own people would kill you. Now whatever game plan you walked in here with has now been shot to hell, and the only play you have left is to try and save your life."

We all sat there and allowed the walls to close in on the Rakehell. "Where is she?" I asked him again, looking at my watch as my phone went off.

"She's in the one place she knows you won't attack."

"Where might that be?"

"Downtown held up in a suite at Greektown."

I shook my head up and down. It made perfect sense to hold up downtown in the heart of Detroit. To attack the casinos would invite law enforcement of every kind.

"So how does this information help me?"

He smiled. "Because she's only held up there at night. They

have an entire floor rented out and they leave before sunrise and head—," he stopped and took off his left shoe. "I knew your boys would not think I'd have the key on me." He held the keycard out to me. Castro took it from his hand.

"Have it checked out," I said.

"Well ladies, this one is yours since my men are out on a mission." Castro gave the address to Ninon.

"What about him?" she said, standing up and Nin did the same.

"He's going to keep me company. Castro will tag along with you, and he'll level the battlefield wherever you need it."

"I'll see you when I see you," Castro said, taking out his Magnum. "Knock him on his ass if you have to." He held out the gun.

He knew I never walked around armed. Carrying a weapon interferes with conflict resolution and problem solving where words can find common ground, but that's lost when a man's ego is inflated by the size of the pistol he carries, and sooner or later you're going to have to yield to that greater power.

Chapter 16

BULLETS WILL FLY WHEN ADRENALINE RUNS HIGH, coupled by the panic in Blast's voice, sent chills down my spine. Bullets could be overheard ricocheting off metal and tearing through flesh by the screams.

"What's your position?" I said, yelling into the phone.

"Manor Street!" he amplified.

"Manor?!" I questioned, because that was not where they were sent to.

"We followed them!" he yelled. "Look man, we chased them down and these bitches got heavy backup. We-- . . . Fuc---. . . Send. . . Help!------"

The line kept breaking up until the call dropped. The Crazy-Eight was a special forces team that met up once they made it back on from overseas and if they were pinned down, Rakehell had to be outnumbering them.

"Let's move," I said to the Rakehell, aka Caveman, as I dialed Castro's number.

"Move where?" Caveman asked, but wasted no time scrambling to his feet and following behind me.

We reached the top landing and bolted out the side door heading for my car.

"What do you know about—" I started to ask Caveman a question when Castro answered his phone.

"What's up, Lion?" he asked.

"Get a team and head to Manor right now?"

"Manor!?" Caveman inquired as he got in the passenger seat. He laughed, "Oh shit, that's a weapons house."

"The Crazy-Eight are pinned down, and our Rakehell says it's a weapons armory."

"We're on our way," Castro said.

"I'm on route."

"You're what?!" Castro yelled, "Lion!". . ."Save it Castro, get your men moving." I hung up.

"You aren't going over there, are you?" Caveman asked.

"Is that a problem?"

"With that piece of shit you carrying? Man, did you hear anything I just said?"

"What you said has these wheels turning."

"God damn!" he yelled.

Then I smiled, as we both witnessed the Wild, Wild West come alive. He slid down in his seat and yelled, "Y'all niggahs got this shit on lock."

As we approached Manor Street, a caravan was forming. Corner after corner, cars were adding up. That was the westside for you, where one call can be made, and a hundred and fifty riders would be at your front door. All of a sudden, riding towards Manor with a single pistol in my lap didn't seem so crazy, but these were my people, and I would have showed up with zip gun if they put out the woo call.

The only time I'd seen a clique come together this strong was when the media would show the military dropping in Iraq with tanks and F15s. "I'm going to need a gun," Caveman said, and the bullets could be heard as we turned the corner onto Manor, where I had to almost swipe a truck due to the light coat of snow on the ground. The block looked like a junkyard full of mangled cars and red slush blood trails dotted the lawns and sidewalks.

"For what?" I finally responded to Caveman's request for a gun.

"You gonna bring me to this death trap empty-handed after what I done told you?!"

I slammed on the brakes. "If you stay put, you're safe. If you step foot out of this car, both sides will gun you down!" I said and as soon as I opened my door and entered the battle, the Tokyo Twins' Range Rover turned the corner on almost two wheels.

My adrenaline kicked in as I saw Blast on the ground gasping for air. The Crazy-Eight's medic was bloody from head to toe, whose blood it was I didn't know but it couldn't have belonged to just one body.

"Help me damn it!" Patch, as he was known yelled out.

"We got to move him!" I yelled, pistol in hand, bullets were hitting cars like heat on popcorn in a microwave, as I kneeled down beside them.

"Put pressure here," he said, lifting his hands soaked in blood.

"Talk to him. Keep him, talking." He was digging in his backpack, and I wondered what he could possibly have in it to save this man from bleeding out to death.

"God damn, he ain't gonna make it," Caveman said, yelling from the passenger seat.

"Open the door!" I yelled. I pointed at Blast, "Here's your way to Arkansas." I jumped up and blew his brains out and got Blast in the car. For every man I lost, a Rakehell was going to die. Patch and I got Blast in the backseat, and I jumped under the wheel.

"We got you baby, don't you let go, fight it!" Patch yelled desperately.

Patch was singing to Blast, "I'm a hard fighting solider, on the battlefield…" "We're on our way to the hospital Blast," I said weaving in and out of traffic.

"Look at me! Don't close your eyes. Look at me, drill sergeant!"

I looked over my shoulder and saw nothing, the only movement was blood leaving Blast's body. I slowed down to the speed limit.

Patch was still trying to save him. "He's gone Patch," I said in a calm voice to get him to sit down in the seat.

"No, no, no!" he denied the obvious. "I got him Lion, just get us to the hospital."

"Get in the front seat," I said. "Blast is dead."

He flopped down in the seat with Blast's corpse. "How many you think we killed back there?"

"More than we lost."

"Then it's a good day to die," he said looking at Blast.

Chapter 17

WE ALL CHOSE OUR DEATHS WHETHER CONSCIOUSLY OR UNCONSCIOUSLY, by the way we live, our habits, and lifestyle choices.

A Covid burial was without the traditional display of flowers, grieving family and friends coming to pay their final respects. With the deaths surpassing 500,000, the people had started to become numb by the gross numbers. Cremation had become more popular due to the long waiting list of the deceased being piled up in trucker storage containers.

All of the city commerce worked hand in hand with the authorities. If you died as was reported, made too much money, or showed up at the emergency ward seeking medical attention from an odd occurrence, it was called in to the police. Blast's body was bullet ridden and I had two choices — to follow his final wishes or turn his body over to his family. There was no way I was going to put his sister through that kind of pain of seeing him for the last time filled with bullet holes. He would be baptized in a bath of acid sodium carbonate NaHCO2, and some other chemicals too long to pronounce. Normally, the responsibility would fall on the O.G.'s to perform, but Blast and I had discussed his final wishes in full detail going back to Boyz n the Hood.

He lived alone in a small playboy furnished red brick house in Lincoln Park. I dropped Patch off at his house and gave Blast one last tour of the city he lived and died for, playing his favorite song by Shyne, "Bad Boyz" before pulling up to his garage and hauling the five-gallon gray paint buckets down to his basement along with three fifty-pound bags of concrete, wheelbarrow, spade shovel, and hoist lift. I used the side door for making the trips back and forth. Took my coat off after the manual labor got my body heated up.

The pit was already there where Blast buried his money, so I dug a hole deep enough to hold his body beneath the basement floor. I opened the five-gallon drums and poured the liquid in to the hole, watched it foam and bubble before bringing Blast down the stairs, removed his jewelry, and dropped him inside the acid grave. The chemicals ate at his shoes, clothes, and flesh as soon as it touched the liquid with a grayish smoke of burnt flesh that turned his blood as black as oil. Before I could release him from my hands, his bones were already exposed to the acid.

Standing there watching his blood turn black became my rage. His eyeballs popped out of their sockets and defied the acid as they hung on to his head by the veins, floating on the surface until they popped like grapes to a fizz just as his fingernails came off one by one bumping into each other until they joined he liquid bubbles. Blast became a skeleton right before my eyes, part of his skull sat up out of the acid leaning to the side.

I looked at the concrete slab hanging by the hoist up to the ceiling and beneath it was a zip lock baggy. I reached up and pulled it away from the duct tape that held it in place and pulled open the zip lock. It was his last will and testament outlining who got what of his property, all the way down to his jewelry, giving most of his life's worth to his sister Kamila and her son Jordan. I folded the documents and put it in my pocket hating I had read it because it meant I had to deliver the news that came along with the will. Afterwards, I mixed and poured the concrete into the pit until nothing remained of Blast's body. I put as much of the dirt I could back in the hole and what would not go I put into the empty buckets and carried them to the car along with the rest of the cleanup. I lowered the concrete slab over the wet concrete and leveled the edges to dry, then swept the floor clean. I knew it would take a while before Kamila actually came to claim the house and if she decided to sell the place, which was her right to choose, the last thing I wanted was anyone nosing around and digging beneath the floor.

Blast had been put to rest, and that was the easy part. The hardest part came with turning out the lights, walking up the stairs and having to deliver the heartbreaking news to Kamila Ross Goodwin that the only brother she entrusted to my care, who on too many occasions to count her words of "don't let anything happen to my brother out in those streets," was a promise I could not keep, would not make it to the next holiday gathering.

Chapter 18

BAD NEWS IS NEVER ACCEPTED WITH OPEN ARMS, especially when the news is delivered by someone who is seen as nothing but trouble. My very first experience of how crazed a rejected woman could become was when I dated Kamila during my predawn years in my efforts to put poverty behind me. A high school fling that she could not get over almost landed me behind bars when she called the police on Blast, myself, and a few other upcoming Lion's when we showed up at her house to celebrate Blast's twenty-first birthday. We all were drunker than a gang of wine-o's and we only drank so hard that night because Blast was legal and wanted to flash his I.D. every place it was required. Kamila did not ask us to leave or to keep the noise down, she just flat out called the cops on us. Fortunately for all of us, Blast started raising so much hell because she had called the police. Not only did it give me enough time to stash my drugs and gun between the pillows of her sofa, but the cops ended up throwing us out of the house to deal with the brother and sister battle.

I hadn't been to her house since that night and vowed I never would step foot there again, and that regret was still with me as I knocked on her door to deliver the bad news of her brother's death.

"Blast ain't here, Lion," Kamila yelled through the door.

I did not know how to even start to deliver the news and just looked at her through the glass.

"Open the door, Kamila," I said. "We need to talk."

She turned on the overhead porch light and looked me over from head to toe, then began hastily unlocking the door.

"What happened to you?" she asked, opening the door and stepping aside to let me in. "Are you shot?"

"No I haven't been shot."

"Then whose blood —" She covered her mouth and took two steps away from me.

I closed the door and every step I took, Kamila backed away from me. I looked down at myself dirty and soiled with blood, then looked back at her.

"I have bad news," I said.

I stepped towards her, and she rushed towards the door. "You have to leave," she said. "Please not my brother."

"I know this —""No... Don't touch me, I don't want your help!" she yelled before breaking down.

All I could do was stand there watching her sob. It was not the first time I had seen Kamila crying, but it was the first time I saw her mourn the loss of her only sibling and that brought a different kind of pain unlike when her tears were over me leaving her. She slid down the door and covered her face so I could not see her tears as her body heaved up and down. I walked over and helped her up from the floor and she violently slapped me and began assaulting me with her fist. "I told you not to let him sell your drugs, now look what you've done!" she screamed as she repeatedly slapped me. "You killed him you murdering bastard! I'll never forgive you."

"I'm sorry, Kamila."

"Fuck your sorry," she said, wiping her tears away. "Your sorry ain't gonna fix nothing but bring everyone pain." Her tears had turned to anger. "Look at you and what you've done!"

I had taken all I could stand and was ready to leave.

"Where is he, take me to him," she said, looking down at herself in her robe. "I have to get dressed."

I stopped her before she could leave the living room. "He's not at any hospital." I touched her shoulder and guided her towards the couch.

"Did you leave him to die alone?"

"I did not leave his side."

"Then take me to him."

"He's gone," I said, and sat down on the sofa.

"What did you do with his body?"

I had not thought it through on telling her she'd never get to lay Blast to rest nor was I going to tell her how I laid him to rest or where I cremated his body.

"We have to call the police," she said.

"No police, Kamila. You have to trust me on this."

"Why should I trust you?!" she yelled, "You can't keep him from me. I'm his only family," she hit her chest, "and you have no right to tell me I can't bury my brother in peace."

The words took the breath from Kamila and she flopped down on the sofa.

"You're going to have to file a missing person report and that's all we can do at this point," I said looking at her.

"Missing person! No, no! You tell me what you did with Blast, or I will tell the police you killed him. I swear to God I'll turn your Black ass in to the police!"

"You'll only cause trouble for yourself and your son Kamila."

"What?! Now you're threatening to kill us?!""No and you know I would not do that. But if you call the cops, you and I both know who paid for this house and almost everything you have. The police will tear your life apart to find out what Blast was into. Now all I can tell you is Blast received the burial he wanted. I did not leave him and he would not want you doing something like calling the police on me for doing what he asked me to do."

I knew Kamila would call the cops in a heartbeat and I was willing to sit there the entire night to convince her that it was the worst option she had.

"How did he die?"

"They shot him," I answered.

"Did he suffer?"

I did not want to answer her question.

"Did he? I deserve to know that much."

"You knew Blast better than anyone," I said, looking into her eyes. "How do you think they had to take him out?"

"Is all that his blood on you?"

"Yeah, I was trying to save him."

My response broke Kamila down again, but this time she leaned over in my arms.

She looked at me and laid her head on my chest. "You go back out there and kill whoever it was that shed his blood and don't you tell me you can't because I know you know who did this."

Laying her head on my chest created discomfort for the both of us because of the bulge in my pocket.

"Here," I said, pulling the contents out of my pocket that was Blast's final will.

She took it and laid the bag on the coffee table. "Tell me you're going to do it."

"It's not possible."

"So you're going to just let them get away with this?"

"No, it's not possible because they're already dead."

I had to tell Kamila the truth and although we had not taken out the entire Rakehell family at that point, we had taken out those responsible for Blast's death. It was more information I wanted to trust in her hands.

"Did he get any of them?"

"He gave as hard as he took."

"And you were there with him?"

"Yeah, he called me and I got there fast as I could."

"Was he alive when you got there?"

"It was a couple of us trying to keep him alive. I got him in the car to get him to the hospital but he died before we could make it."

She looked at me. "He loved you, you know?"

"I know, but he loved you more."

"You think so?" she asked. "Just seemed like the streets had a better pull on him no matter what I said to him."

"Well, all I remember is being hit in the mouth in high school for making you cry about whatever it was you told him. Now which one of us do you think he loved more?"

Kamila laughed. "Oh no, you don't remember that," she continued laughing.

"Bullshit," I said. "I skipped school for a week until my big ass lip went down, and you put him on me."

"No I did not, Lion. He made me tell him why I was crying."

Kamila and I sat there until sunrise reminiscing and telling each other stories one after another about Blast until I presented her with one last request.

"He wanted you to have this," I said, handing her the will. "He left you the house, both cars, and a few other investments that will take care of you and his nephew. Some of which we have invested in together."

"Can we just deal with this later. I mean, maybe you can come by and help me understand it all."

"Ah yeah okay, I can do that."

"Yeah because," she pointed down at my bloody clothes, "I don't want my son to see you with —""Yeah, you're right," I stood up to leave

.Death was strange in a way that it had a way of bringing even the hated and despised together to settle our differences over issues held onto for decades. Kamila carried the burden of a woman scorned from high school, but Blast's death put life in perspective. Although I had no room for being around anyone who used the long arm of the law to settle disputes, I felt I owed it to Blast to make sure Kamila and her son was taken care of. I hoped when my day came, those around me would do the same for those I provided for. That plus, the letter taped to the will read in part: "If you're in my basement reading this Lion, it means I'm dead. Look out for big sis for me. See you on the other side — Blast."

Chapter 19

"BIG DAWG!" RANDI GARNICK'S OF AMERICAN AUTO Parts (a junkyard) nephew said, climbing out of his F250 truck. "Ain't seen you in a while. What you need?"

"Got a little clean up job for you," I said, tapping two fingers on the trunk of the car.

"No shit," he said, red eyed.

"Got to be today."

He squinted his eyes to study what I was asking of him.

"What you working with, Big Dawg?" he asked.

"Triple-A will cover my end, everything else is yours."

"Word?" he said, and looked over at the front door of the auto parts shop then back at me. "System still good?"

"Only one hitch."

"Ah shit," he got dramatic. "This bitch ain't on the hot sheet, is it?"

"No, nothing like that."

He looked in the backseat and almost walked away. "What you do, Big Dawg? Kill a motherfucker in the backseat?"

"I lost a homie, but it can't come back to me."

"What am I supposed to do if the cops come looking for this car?"

"It's going to be your ass because I've already filed a stolen report on it."

"Oh hell no, I don't know about this one baby. This is some heavy gangster shit you pulling on me."

"It's simple," I said. "Just don't go joyriding in it."

"How much?" he asked, pocketing the money I passed him without looking at it.

"Does it matter?"

"Wait here, okay?" He rushed into the parts shop.

Moments later, the double chain fence opened and Brent came rushing out towards me. "Okay, give me the keys."

I handed him the keys. "I don't have to tell you this, but I will. If you fuck this up and my name comes up on a police report, I'll deny ever knowing you and we'll have unfinished business between us."

"Come on Big Dawg, have I ever crossed you before?"

"Strip it bare and burn anything with blood on it," I said, walking away.

"You don't have a ride?" he asked, jumping in the driver's seat.

"City's full of transportation," I said, waving goodbye to him and the car.

⟨⟨⟨⟩⟩⟩

I had called an Uber and was waiting on my driver to arrive when a car pulled up next to me and rolled the window down. "Are you Lion?" he asked. "Yeah, that's me," I responded.

"Man, you look like this dude I used to go to high school with," the Uber driver said. "You ever attend Mumford?"

"No," I said flatly.

"You know any Peterson's, 'cause you could be Gibson Peterson's brother."

I looked out the passengers window without responding. As far as I was concerned our conversation ended once he put my address into the GPS. What do I look like telling a stranger all my business?

"Right here is fine," I said to the Uber driver once I was in walking distance from my Grosse Pointe home.

I got out of the Uber at the corner of Kelly Road, flipped my collar up around my ears and started walking in the opposite direction from where the Uber driver was heading until he was out of sight.

Chapter
20

THE INAUGURATION OF PRESIDENT-ELECT JOE BIDEN and the historic Vice President-Elect Kamala Harris was heading to Washington, D.C., amidst domestic threats on all fifty state capitals by extremist. It seemed nowhere was safe and death was in full bloom.

There was no mention of the shooting deaths on the news, not a single word. After making it home, I took a shower to wash the blood of war off my body, grabbed a bottle of Hennessey, and poured a tall glass before taking out the cigar that held the Valentino's family ring. I clipped the end of the cigar, lit it, and processed the day along with contemplating my next move. If you asked me how that worked out, as usual my next move was dictated by speed of time. And like the Covid-19 pandemic, as soon as I thought I had a vaccine and everything's under control, a variant pops up and its mutation is resistant to my efforts to bring life back to normal. Which could prove itself catastrophic for the Lion family if I made a miscalculation in my decision making. I could have followed that thought to the bottom of my Hennessey bottle and probably would have until my phone vibrated on the coffee table in front of me.

I looked at the screen to see who was calling. "Hello."

"I'm mad at you," Medina said in my ear.

"Get in line and take a number," I responded. Hearing her voice brought a smile to my face.

"Why haven't you been answering your phone?"

"My bad, I've had a busy day."

"So where are you laying your head, if you don't mind me asking?"

"One of my side pieces' houses."

"Ha-ha, Lion," Medina laughed. "You must want to get cut or are you just being an asshole?"

"This is new," I said, studying the details in the Legion ring.

"Not answering my calls is new."

"I was going to call you back when I got out of the shower."

"I called you earlier and one of your flunkies answered. Why would someone named Castro be answering your phone?"

Castro told me that Ferrell called but never mentioned Medina calling, which caught me off guard.

"His battery died and I let him use my phone and when we separated, I forgot to get it back from him," I answered, taking a sip of Hennessey.

"Huh-uh."

"You say that like you don't believe me."

"Does it matter?"

"Yes it does."

"Bye Lion, I just called because I was worried when I haven't heard from you and wanted to know if you were okay."

"I am sorta," I said.

"What does sorta mean Lion?"

"A friend of mine was killed last night."

I had to say something to account for why I had not been home or answering my phone.

"Lion honey," she said in a concerned tone. ""I'm so sorry to hear that. Why didn't you tell me?"

"I didn't want to worry you."

"Were you there when it happened?"

"Sorta," I said.

"That means you were there."

"This is why I didn't want to tell you."

"What is it you don't want to tell me, that I shouldn't worry about you hanging around people being killed?"

Another call came in. "Hold on a minute, I have to take this," I said, switching lines.

I clicked over, happy for the interruption because Medina was an Aries (ram) and turned everything into a challenge or battle, and wasn't going to back down.

"Hello."

"Miss me?" Ferrell asked.

I sat up in my chair, "How was your flight?"

"It was fine but that does not answer my question."

"You fucked up my house," I said in response to her question.

"Really, what did I do wrong?"

"I'm at my Grosse Pointe retreat and I'm afraid your presence has affected the place."

She laughed uncontrollably. "I'll accept that as a yes."

"Look, I have someone on hold, hold on a second and let me clear the line, okay?"

"The service here is bad so if the call drops, I'll call you right back."

"Alright hold on," I switched lines. "Hello."

"I'm here," Medina said.

"This is an overseas call, I'll call you after I wrap this up.""Who do you know overseas?

"An investment partner."

"Shut up! Okay, Mr. Businessman, sounds important."

"It is. I'll call you back."

"Why don't you come for dinner and give me the details."

"I don't know if I can make dinner."

"Call me back, Lion."

Medina hung up before I could say anything else and there was definitely attitude in her voice over me turning down dinner. I waited a minute then clicked to the other line.

"I'm back," I said.

"And I waited for you."

"So how's everything going over there?" I asked and feeling a little guilty that I put Medina off like I had.

"Great," Ferrell said. "I may be coming back sooner than I thought. Turns out all they wanted was, you know," she giggled.

"Damn! You got the old men bowing down to you?"

"Oh my goodness, it was so embarrassing. You have no idea."

"So when do you think you'll be stateside?"

"I really can't say for sure because they have some others coming in who I must meet and one of their flights has been delayed. And they have this big thing being set up in my honor that can't start until everyone is here."

"Sounds big. Congratulations, Ms. Valentino."

"Thank you, honey."

"You're very welcome."

"No, really, I wanted to thank you for preparing me for this. I could not have done any of this without you."

"Somehow I think you would have done just fine without me."

"Oh please, remember that little talk we had with your friend pressing me?"

I laughed.

"Yeah, I remember."

"Well, you were right about what you said afterwards, and I used it to broker a new deal for us. Oh, and before I forget, did you know you're known as the Lionheart of Africa over here"?"

No, I never heard that before."

I was more than impressed with the idea of being associated with the continent of Africa even though I had never been there.

"Yes," Ferrell started. "They have all kinds of stories about you over here, it appears I wasn't the only one Andrew talked to about you."

"Hello?" I said due to the bad reception.

"Lion, can you hear me?" Ferrell said through bad static.

"Yeah but you're breaking up."

"Oh noo-o-o-o!" Her words extended.

"We better end before we're completely cut off," I said, wondering if my words were breaking up like hers were.

"I miss you," came clearly over the line.

"Miss you, too."

"Bye."

I hung the phone up thinking of how tired my body felt until I received the back-to-back calls. I wanted to go see Medina. No, I needed to see her and to try to explain my new relationship with Ferrell. But I knew that that would only complicate matters further and that she would not accept knowing that another woman was on my line which meant that there would come times where she would have to share space with another lioness

.This was not the wild kingdom where the lion ruled over as many lionesses as he could protect. Ferrell had made it known that what was my business was my business as long as I did not flaunt it in front of her and although she was willing to accept things on those terms, Medina would not stand for the 'my business is my business' when it came to Ferrell.

I drank the last of the cognac from my glass as I waited for Medina to pick up her phone. It had already rung five times that told me I was heading towards a confrontation. If not about being in the company of Blast when he was killed, surely skipping out on dinner with her would be an issue. The Christmas holidays was in two days' time and not only was it a bad time of the year to be alone, but it was equally bad to be around people. I had not even slowed down to get her any gifts nor help her put up and decorate the tree that I normally would make time to be by her side, even if I just sat there drinking eggnog spiked with brandy and watched her go through the motions of the holiday spirit.

"Hello," she answered just as I was about to hang up.

"What you doing?" I asked.

"I was waiting for you to come help me decorate the tree but since you're so damn busy, I decided to do it alone. And you tangled up my lights putting them away last year, and you know I don't have patience for this sort of stuff."

"I'm sorry about that."

"About what, screwing up my lights or messing up my holiday plans?"

"Look Medina, I didn't call to argue with you. Things are crazy for me right now and I'll be over there as soon as I can make it."

"And when will that be, after you chased down the people who killed your friend? And what's it going to change once you find them? You're going to destroy the meaning of this season for their families? Isn't one family grieving enough? I'm sorry about your friend Lion but is revenge the answer?"

"You know I've been really having a problem trying to figure out what to get you for Christmas," I said to change the subject. "I mean, after you made such a big deal about your birthday gifts."

"Wait! Stop, stop, damn it!" she shouted, "Don't do that and just dismiss what I just said to you as if what I'm saying is of no importance! You answer my questions or I'm going to hang this fuckin phone up in your face."

"What do you want me to say, Medina? That I'm not upset

or because it's Christ's birthday, I'm in a goddamn forgive-thy-neighbor mood? I had to deliver the bad news to my friends' family that her brother is dead, and now she hates me for being the messenger of death, and all you can talk about is tangled Christmas lights."

"You know what? Fuck you, Lion! Yeah, I said fuck you and your bullshit street war! I don't want any part of any gifts you have to offer me from money you've earned from hurting people."

"You need to take a deep breath girl because you're crossing a thin line with that smart mouth," I said.

"Or what?!" she yelled, and I could hear her throwing something in the background. "What are you going to do, Big Badass?! Put me in my place?!""I think we better end this phone call before we both say something we'll regret later," I said, trying to compose myself.

"Yeah right! Do what you're best at, avoiding issues you are not in control over. And you know what? I've been taking deep breaths and I'm tired of having to take them every time I watch the news and see things I know you're a part of or has your signature trademarks on it. So, don't tell me to take a deep breath because I can't take worrying about you every time you leave this house to go out there to be with those ignorant fools."

We all have our boiling points and Medina had reached hers. She was saying far more than I had realized she paid attention to. Like the news and the activities taking place in the inner city.

"Goodbye Medina," I said.

"You better not hang this phone up in my face!" she said angrily.

"I tell you what, I'm on my way there because I don't like my business being aired over the phone."

"Well then bring your badass on over here you motherfucker cause I ain't scared of your Black ass!"

I laughed, not from humor but frustration. "Girl you are out of control."

"Bye Lion!" She slammed the phone down in my ear.

If it was her plan to provoke a face to face, then it worked because I was on my way as always with ten toes in the game. Only a strong woman can move a rock, and I was a rolling stone.

Chapter 21

THIS WAS MY FIRST TIME I EVER USED MY KEYS TO enter Medina's house, after we had just engaged in our first falling out over my line of work. Usually when she knew I was coming, she'd meet me at the door, or it would be unlocked. I let myself in fully prepared to walk back out without the keys on my keychain.

"Here," Medina said, sitting on the floor in the living room in front of a nine-foot-tall pine Christmas tree with her back to the door. "I've been sitting here for hours trying to untangle these things," she said in her calm level voice, with a glass of eggnog next to a bag of ornaments. "Don't just stand there burning a hole in the back of my head," she said, still without looking back at me.

I was so dumbfounded all I could do was laugh.

"What's so funny?" she asked. "I know it's a silly thing to do but I just want to have something to unwrap."

I took the lights to untangle them and paused from trying

to get a knot out that I was sure I didn't put them away that mangled.

Medina was on her second glass of eggnog and brandy to my first mug.

"You're just going to sit there not speaking to me?" she asked, then got up off the floor, pulled her dress up and climbed in my lap. "I know you came here to do battle for what I said on the phone, but I was upset, and I was just venting out to you. But I'm not your enemy, trust me I'm not." She hugged me, "I guess sometimes it's too much and I have to stop bringing all of my issues on you but I'm a girl, all you had to do was let me say what I needed to get off my chest without trying to correct me."

I leaned back on the sofa and closed my eyes for the first time in what seemed like a week.

"Lion, say something baby," Medina laid her head on my shoulder. "Will it help if I said I'm sorry for everything I said?"

"I think we're going to have to buy some more lights," I said, finally speaking.

Medina lifted her head from my shoulder and laughed. "Does that mean you forgive me?"

"It means you need to get off me so I can go to the mall and be around a bunch of super spreaders."

"No," she said. "Not until you say you forgive me."

I motioned to get up and Medina wrapped her arms tightly around my neck. "No! No-o-o!" She was half laughing and half screaming. "Plus I'm horny."

"It's going to have to wait until I get back."

"What about a quickie?" she said, reaching down between her legs to unzip my zipper as she kissed me.

I accepted the kiss, but pulled her hand away from my zipper that turned into a tug of war.

"A quickie means I'll have to shower afterwards which I don't have time to do."

"You didn't say you were going shopping."

"You still have gifts to wrap?"

"Yes. But I need to pick up a few more gifts, so I'll go with you," she said, climbing from my lap, and grabbing my penis. "You might not want a quickie but look who does."

"You're not going with me, Medina." I moved her hand to stop her from getting me harder.

"Why not?"

"A gift is supposed to be a surprise, not you pointing out what you want me to get you."

"I wouldn't do that."

"Like you didn't do last year?"

She laughed. "Will you let that go."

"Fine," I said, walking past her.

"Wait," she said. "Can I have a kiss to hold me over?"

I ran my hands down both sides of her hips and stuck my tongue in her mouth while running my hands down her thighs and pulling her dress up.

"I thought you wanted to wait for it." She grabbed my hands from getting her dress up past her hips. While rubbing her hips, I realized she had no panties on, and the idea of a quickie seemed all the more interesting.

"I did," I said, responding to Medina's remark.

"Then stop being a nasty boy trying to run your hands up my dress."

"If I don't make it back, you may have to come bail me out."

"What, why?"

I looked down at my pants. "You think if the cops pull me over and see I'm carrying a concealed weapon they're going to let me get off with a warning?"

Medina looked down and laughed. "You are so stupid. Bye, Lion," She began pushing me out the door. "You better not rat me out and tell them I gave you that weapon."

⚬≡≡≡⚬

Summerset Mall was unusually packed but not surprisingly so around the holidays. Online shopping due to Covid had nearly bankrupt the stores, but none of that got in the way of the new generation. They came out to shop, meet up, and to rebel against Covid and the security guards that tried to get them to keep their mask worn above their chins.

Inside the mall, I was at a loss on what to get for Medina.

"Excuse me," I said, walking up to a total stranger, a beautiful well developed young woman who was perhaps in her early to mid-twenties and was doing some serious shopping in the lingerie section at Victoria's Secret.

I liked her right off the bat and more so when she turned around to face me with a satin purple butterfly top and lace panties in her hands.

"I apologize for intruding on what clearly is a delicate art you're engaged in," I said, "but I was observing you from afar and I was wondering if you could help me pick out a few nice things for my woman who is about your identical shape and size," I said, noticing the look on her face. "These clerks are only out to make a sale and because they're so busy, they can't spare the time I need them to provide to help me pick out gifts." I went inside my pocket and thumbed through a band. "I'll pay you for your time, if this isn't enough."

"What is it you're looking for?" she said, eyeing the money in my hand and turning around to put the lingerie back on the clothing rack, and turning back around to giving me her undivided attention.

With money in one hand, I extended the other. "I'm Lion."

"Je'Niece," she responded, shaking my hand.

"Well, Je'Niece," I said, "today you're going to be shopping for two." I let go of her hand. "In return for your generosity, I'm going to treat you to whatever you want, starting with that ideal piece of lingerie you just hung up. Get it, it's yours."

"Are you serious?" Je'Niece asked, looking around as if she were being pranked.

"If you pick out a red outfit for yourself, I want you to pick out something for my woman of the same style, but it doesn't necessarily have to be the same color. You're about the same height and size so everything should fit her. I can't be sure of your breast size because of your jacket but I'm sure —"Je'Niece unzipped her sleeveless bomber jacket to show her top curves beneath her purple studded Divine Diva hoodie.

She blushed as she held her jacket open for my viewing. "Is she this size?" Je'Niece stuck her breast up and turned sideways.

"Those are nice, I mean yeah."

She then laughed. "You want me to try something on for you to see?"

"It's totally up to you."

"I like to try on things before I buy them because if it doesn't fit, then I have to come all the way back to exchange it." She then examined another piece of lingerie in pink. "You're going to have to trust me on this one because we don't know each other well enough for me to be giving you a fashion show in this."

"I think we both might go to jail if you came out of that booth in that piece."

"I'll be right back," Je'Niece said and headed for the private booth with her hips swinging from side to side.

I browsed the other clothing racks while she changed and reappeared smiling her own approval.

"I like this one," she said. "What do you think?"

"Very nice."

"Good, but you have to tell me what else you want."

"Everything."

"Everything, just what does that mean?"

I pulled out a rubber band from both pockets. Je'Niece mouth fell open. "You can't be serious. Is this a joke, because if it is and you have me trying on all this stuff making me look like a fool, I swear—"I walked up to Je'Niece and put one knot in her hand. "I don't play games," I said. "When you've spent all of that, then we'll start on this one. I'm Christmas shopping Je'Niece, what would you think of your man if he brought one gift under the tree for you?"

"I ain't gonna even ask what it is you do for a living to be able to spend this kind of money on a stranger." She pointed a credit card at me, "Here I am maxing out my cards to buy myself a Christmas gift 'cause no one else was gonna buy me anything and you show up out of nowhere spending money like it grew on trees. And you're right about one thing," she said as I followed behind her.

"What's that?" I asked.

"You don't play."

"By the way, I need to pick up some lights," I said after spotting a showcase of Christmas lights. "What about you?"

"No, our tree has enough stuff on it."

Je'Niece went in one store after another picking out gifts for Medina and herself, would look at the price tags, at me and then purchase the item. She designated me the bags' holder.

"I feel almost embarrassed to ask you this, but since this is my money and your girlfriend's, I was wondering if I could buy something for you from the both of us," she said.

"Why don't you keep whatever it is you have for yourself to pay down some of your bills or your credit cards?"

Je'Niece dropped one of the many bags from her hands and was followed by another. "Oh shit," she said, her hands as well as my own too filled to pick them up.

"Let me help you," the lady behind the cologne glass counter said as she came to lend a helping hand. "Oh my, are you okay?"

she inquired as she tried to find a place to put the bag in Je'Niece hands."No," Je'Niece said dropping her head.

I stepped closer to her side. "You alright?"

"I'm okay, this is just a lot."

"Thank you," Je'Niece said to the clerk who returned to her station. "I never spent this much money on myself at a time, and I just wanted to do something for you."

"You saved my ass with what you picked out here, and that's a gift by itself. I feel I still owe you more because you won't be there to reap the rewards of this day, but I will."

We pushed through the double glass doors and out into the crisp night air.

"Where's your car?" I asked, looking around for where I had parked myself.

"I don't have one. Well, I do but it starts when it wants to."

"Then how did you get here?"

"I came with some friends and we were supposed to meet back up but I got caught up with you doing all this shopping and lost track of time."

"I'm right here," I said as I deactivated the alarm.

"Wow!" Je'Niece exclaimed. "Oh no, you not driving my car!"

I began tossing the bags into the backseat. "I hope you remember which ones belong to me and which ones are yours," and noticed she was just standing there. "You gonna put those in the back or hold onto them?"

"You've been nice enough. I can catch an Uber."

"I would feel guilty leaving you out here after I caused you to miss your ride. And besides it's too dangerous out in these streets carrying that many bags."

Je'Niece tossed her bags in the backseat and got in the front seat.

⌒〰〰〰⌒

IT'S A SMALL WORLD. . . The ride to Je'Niece's home was further out than I had anticipated. She lived in an area that I was very familiar with.

"My mother is going to like you," Je'Niece said, separating her bags from that of Medina's.

"Your mother," I asked, looking directly at their home. "Who said I was going to meet your mother?"

"You'll see, she's a trip."

"So where do you live?"

"Do you know how to get to Puritan and Cherrylawn?"

"Cherrylawn, by Marygrove College?"

"Yeah," she answered, looking at me with a puzzled expression on her face as I pulled into traffic.

"What's that look for?"

"Nothing," she said, but I knew it was something. She just wasn't saying what it was, and maybe she was just considering her safety which I could not blame her for being cautious.

Whatever it was that sparked the look by Je'Niece had caused her to remain quiet for most of the drive to Cherrylawn. The only reason I did not press her for a response was because there was not a bad vibe, that and the fact that I was almost sure that she had heard of me and perhaps it was not until we got into my car, and she asked was I familiar with where she lived. Je'Niece was definitely too young to have been around in my youthful years in making my come up on Puritan, but she was old enough to have heard my name being in circulation on the streets. Then again, I didn't know how long she had lived in the area.

Chapter 22

IF I SAID IT ONCE, I'LL SAY IT AGAIN: JE'NIECE WAS definitely too young to have been around when I was getting it out the mud on the westside of Puritan, but not her mother.

"Lion!" Kelly (aka Suga) Slanton let out a loud scream as she did a little dance. "Lord, I wouldn't believe it if I wasn't here to see you in the flesh."

"Wait, y'all know each other?" Je'Niece asked. "How you doing, Suga?" I asked.

"Yeah we know each other girl, but what I want to know is where y'all know each other from," Suga put a hand on her hip.

"We met at the mall, he brought me all these gifts to help him do some shopping for his girlfriend, and he brought me home."

Suga laughed. "You're still the same old Lion, come on in and put that stuff down."

"Thanks," I said after my hands were free.

"I don't get a hug or something," Je'Niece's mother said as

she closed in to hug me. "I see you still the neighborhood Robin Hood."

"I'm going to get the rest of my gifts out the car," Je'Niece said.

Suga moved in and took my arm and wrapped her arms around my arm.

"She looks like you," I said, watching Je'Niece leave out the door.

"Man, where did you disappear to Lion?"

"I never left."

"So all the rumors I've been hearing is true?"

"Depends on what's being said," I said, watching Je'Niece re-enter the house with her remaining gifts.

Suga let go of my arm.

"Do you need my help or is that everything?" I asked.

"No that's it," Je'Niece responded.

Suga shot a look at Je'Niece and then back at me as if she was attempting to read the both of us. I had just met Je'Niece and knew far less about her than I knew her mother and if I could read the discontent on her face, I assumed her mother could as well.

"Come on and have a seat, Lion," Suga said, preparing to sit down herself.

"Thank you for the gifts and a ride home," Je'Niece said, "I'll let you two catch up on old times."

"No thank you," I said to Suga offering me a seat. "I won't be staying," was meant for the both of them, "and you're welcome for the gifts."

"Oh okay,"

Suga said with disappointment.

Je'Niece unfolded her arms and smiled, "I'll walk you to your car."

"It was good to see you," I said to Suga.

"Hu hu," she responded, coming in for another hug. "You better come by and visit me now that you know where I live." She rubbed my chest after letting go of the hug.

"I will," I said, then let her go. "Happy holidays."

"Happy holidays to you too, honey."

"She gets on my nerves," Je'Niece said once we were out on the front porch and she followed me down the steps to my car.

"Mothers tend to do that," I said, as I unlocked the doors. "But her getting on your nerves just gives you the patience to deal with the chaos of this world."

I opened the passenger's door. "You want to chill out a few minutes before going back inside?"

"Yeah," she said, and I closed the door once she was seated, climbed in the driver's seat, and turned the engine over to knock the chill off Je'Niece attitude.

"I got to tell you something," she said after a few minutes of silence.

"I already know."

"Shut up," she said. "What was I going to say?"

"At some point back at the mall, it hit you who I was," I smiled.

"How did you know?" she said, excitingly.

"Your silence. People tend to say more by their silence than when we're talking," I said, while putting on my leather driving gloves.

Je'Niece was someone I liked. She could look me straight in the eyes and communicate how she felt without masking her intentions.

"Are you going to ask for my number?" she asked. "And you better not say I'm too young just because you know my momma. I'm twenty-six and old enough to like you."

"And you don't think I'm too old for you?" I asked, and was strongly thinking about calling her.

"If I thought you didn't have no swagger, I would not have gotten in your car a second time."

"Look at me."

"I am looking at you."

"No, I don't want you to see the person that's rumored of in the streets," I said. "I want you to see me as I am."

"Okay, now that's deep."

"Yeah, but what's even more deep is what I'm about to tell you," I started. "With me, there are no secrets. You've heard the rumors, now let me bear the truth so you know what you're dealing with. I am the heaviest hitter on these streets, and perhaps the most dangerous person you'll ever meet. People die when I say they die, and although this life is filled with diamonds, mansions, fast cars, and so much money I use money machines to count it all. You're a very attractive woman and have your whole life ahead of you to become a superstar wherever you go. You should avoid men like me because in my world, you'll be dragged down to my level, and there will be no way out nor for you to hide once you invite someone like me into your life. Because you'll learn and see too much to be allowed to walk away. In my world, death is the only out. That said, now all you must do is open that door and follow another path, but if you hang on my arm beyond this point of knowing more than you should, then there may come a point where I can't let you leave."

Je'Niece paused and said, "Does that still mean you're not going to ask me for my number?" She looked at me, "Because I want yours if you're not going to ask. And I didn't say I was going to do anything illegal for you because I'm not. I just think it would be nice for us to hang out with each other from time to time. You can just call me when you just want to do something private and special. I don't want to meet your friends or take up all your time, just some of it."

I shook my head from side to side. "I have a few women for that already," I said, trying to resistant her temptation.

"Then they can't be that good because if they were, you wouldn't need that many."

I laughed, then took a pen and piece of paper from the glove compartment.

"What's your number?"

"Yeah right, don't you have an iPhone 12?"

"Yeah, you can have my number."

"Let me see it."

I went into my pocket and handed Je'Niece my iPhone.

"This way it won't get blown in the wind."

"You have my number as well."

"Well, you better call me because," Je'Niece patted her pocket, tapping her phone, "I don't like to be put on hold."

"Enjoy your holidays."

"Yeah and that," she said, "what's her name?" She tilted her head towards the gifts in the back.

"Medina."

"I like that, Medina."

"Goodbye Je'Niece."

"Bye Lion," she said, getting out of the car. "I want to celebrate the New Year with you after you're done with Medina," and closed the door before I could respond.

I sat there until Je'Niece got in the house, thinking women aren't as fragile as they are made out to be. They are curiously attracted to the forbidden fruit, danger, and living on the edge. I pulled off anticipating our next encounter before I bent the corner.

Chapter
23

SURVIVAL OF THE FITTEST IS THE ABILITY TO ADAPT to any given situation at any given moment under any circumstances, no matter what you come up against, and to do whatever is necessary without reservation over the perceived outcome despite the end results.

By the time I left Je'Niece and made it back to Medina's driveway, I noticed before parking that the front door was wide open. As I got out of the car, my first thought as I was about to grab some of her gifts was that she saw me coming and opened the door for me as she usually did, but not as wide open. I could see inside from where I stood, broken porcelain, the turned over parlor table, flowers that sat on the table, picture frame, as I rushed into the house.

"Medina!" I yelled, stepping into the ransacked house and to my shock, everything had been turned upside down.

"Medina!" I called out. "Are you here?!"

A small sniffle came from behind the overturned Christmas

tree. I rushed in crushing the Christmas bulbs beneath my shoes and the popping caused Medina alarm. She was curled up in a fetus position behind the tree having been assaulted. I bent over to pull the tree away from her and pulling it up, I was startled to discover a bloody body beneath the tree with half of the star of David that was intended for the top of the tree lodged in the attacker's neck, the other half was still in Medina's bloody hand. Her clothes badly torn and I couldn't tell if all of the blood was from dead guy or from the both of them.

I tossed the tree off to the side and stepped over the ski masked corpse to help Medina up.

"Please! . . . Please no!" she screamed and prepared to defend herself against my help. I jumped back. "Medina it's me, Lion."

"Lion!?" She looked up, dropped the weapon and tried to get off the floor.

"Wait babe, I got you. I got you." I rushed down to take her in my arms.

"Oh my God, I didn't know what to do. I thought I forgot something and when I turned around, they attacked me." Medina was squeezing my neck so hard she was choking me.

"It's okay," I said. "Just calm down."

"No!" She started kicking and swinging to put her down. "PUT ME DOWN! No!" she was yelling.

There were no words to describe the moment or what I was feeling at that point. All I could do was get her out of the house and into my car until I could get her nerves calm enough for me to think. When I got her to the car, she wouldn't let me put her down, so I had to put her in the driver's seat.

"Slide over baby," I said, but she didn't move, just began rocking back and forth mumbling something incoherent.

"Medina," I knelt inside of the doorway, "can you hear me honey bunny?"

"Is he dead?" she asked, looking at the blood on her hands. "Is this my blood or is this his blood all over me?"

"That doesn't matter right now."

"Yes it does, I think I killed him."

"Okay, keep it down baby. I need you to slide over so I can get in the car with you."

When Medina slid over, I saw that she had cuts under her feet, her panties were ripped and hanging on by a thread. She tried to straighten her clothes when she was in the passenger's seat.

I looked down at her. "I have to go back inside for a minute okay?"

Medina stared at me as if she was lost in a trance.

"Medina, did you hear me?"

"I just need to get away from here."

"Okay, I just need one minute and we'll leave."

I closed the door, pulled out my phone and headed into the house to call Castro.

"This better be important," he said answering the phone.

"It is," I said walking into the living room towards the dead body. "Lion, Wassup?... I thought you were—"

"Never mind all that. We have a situation at Medina's," I said, kneeling down next to the dead body and pulling the ski mask off the attackers head. "Shit," and stood back up looking down at him.

"What's the deal?" Castro asked.

"Send a cleaner."

"At Medina's?"

"Yeah, looks like Rakehell tagged me."

"You sure it's them?"

"Looking at the pitch-fork and skull tattoo on his neck."

"Okay wait, did Medina see the whole thing?"

I paused. "Negative, I wasn't here."

"Oh shit, you're not telling me she—""Just get this cleaned up," I said, grabbing Medina's purse, her coat, and keys off the floor as I headed for the door.

"Goddamn, okay I'm on it just get out of there."

"No, I don't want you on this one," I said, pulling the door shut. "This is a neighborhood watch community and strange faces draw attention. Use our New York Carpet World cleaner crew with the Crazy-Eight."

"Got it."

"And Castro?"

"Yeah."

"Get everybody down to the Brotherhood."

"Now?"

"Now Castro, now!"

"I hear you man (pause), but you know it will be open in a few hours?"

"Then that means you have a tight window to operate in. Tell the Eights the keys are in a Manila envelope in the mailbox, and send Jesse to my place in Ferndale," I said and ended the call and got in the car.

"Is he dead?" Medina asked again as I backed out of the driveway.

"Why don't you just let me handle everything," I said, not wanting to say anything that would have her creating a scene as we left and draw attention to us leaving.

"I'm not a child, Lion! I was defending myself in my own home. All I asked you is. . . is that bastard dead!?"

"He's dead."

Long silence.

"No, how do you know. Did you check to see if he had a pulse? I wasn't trying to kill him, just to stop them."

"Them, you keep saying they and them. So, there was more than him?" I was focused on the road as ice patches appeared every so often, but also trying to get as much intel out of Medina while she was now coherent.

"Three, there were three of them."

"You fought off three men?"

"It was two men and a nasty bitch!"

"Okay, okay, I got it," I said and Medina became aggressive over my questioning her. "Just calm down, everything's being taken care of."

"How can you say that when I just killed a man. I'm not YOU!"

"What's that supposed to mean?"

"It means you can't fix what I've done by sweeping it under the carpet, and walk away as if nothing happened, I have a conscience."

We hit the 96 Expressway and Medina's comments seemed to pick up with my speed and the faster I drove the sharper her insults rose.

"It means I'm not a killer like you are!"

"No, you're not," I said, biting my lip.

"But now because of you I am."

"Because of me?"

"Don't try to play me Lion!" she yelled. "That vicious woman asked for you by trademark and name. Now I want to know which one of your whores did you bring to my house."

"I did not bring anyone to your house Medina," I said. "Now clearly you're upset but—""Upset is not the word to describe what I am! I was almost raped! And there's a dead man lying on my living room floor. Upset doesn't begin to describe what I am, and you know what? I want out of this damn car and to get far away from you as possible. I've tolerated your bullshit for as long as you kept it away from me, now—" She looked around. "Where are you taking me, we should be going to the police precinct and tell them what happened back there to clear myself and not be out here on the run like I did something wrong."

Medina ranted and raved all the way across town and for a minute I thought she was capable of opening the door and jumping out onto the freeway in moving traffic. She was beyond right and the more I tried to calm her down the more enraged she became, and going to the police station ended our conversation.

I pulled into the driveway of my second home in Ferndale, and was my first choice because it was the only house Medina knew of.

"You'll be safe here until I get back," I said, looking in my rearview mirror as Jesse got out of his car and was coming to the car.

"You're going to leave me here alone?!" Medina was preparing to get started again, "If I'm not safe in my own house from people looking for you, what in the hell makes you think I'll be safe where you live?"

"Because if they wanted you dead, you would be dead. They wanted to send me a message."

Medina was so fixed on attacking me she didn't see Jesse walk up to the window and practically scared the hell out of her when he tapped on the window.

It was the only thing that calmed her down.

"Who is that!?" she asked after almost climbing in my lap.

"That's Jesse," I lowered the window. "He'll be looking after you until I get back."

"Lion," he said, looking inside. "Sorry, didn't mean to startle you. I would get in but looks like you're full."

Medina turned to see what Jesse was referring to. "Are those mine?" she asked.

"Yeah, you're going to have to open them early to find you something to wear," I said getting out of the car.

"I can't let him see me like this, Lion."

"Yeah, why don't I pull into the garage and he'll come in behind us."

"Okay."

"Let me get her inside and we can get her things out," I pulled my leg back inside and pushed the garage opener.

Jesse shook his head up and down then backed away for the car.

Once the garage door was opened, I pulled inside and let the door back down, got out and opened the door that led into the kitchen. Medina went ahead of me upstairs as I hit the switch to reopen the door. Jesse helped me bring the gifts into the living room. We made a couple trips apiece and I grabbed a few things and took them up to Medina, knocking softly on the bedroom door before entering the room.

"Yes."

"It's me, can I come in? I have some clothes for you to wear."

"Come in."

"The rest is in the living room if you don't like these."

She took them from my hand. "I can't believe you're going to leave me here with a stranger."

"I trust Jesse with my life, and he'll give his to protect you."

"That's the problem, everybody around you is willing to die for you."

"I'm sorry for what's happened and as much as I want to comfort you right now, there are people on the streets on a killing spree that has to be stopped."

"Hand me a towel," she said, and went into the bathroom.

I walked into the bathroom with her and pulled a towel from the rack and handed it to her. She took her clothes off and tossed everything she took off into the waste paper basket next to the sink, before stepping into the tub and easing down into the bubbles.

"We'll talk about this when I get back."

"No we won't," Medina looked up at me. "Just leave your keys on the nightstand on your way out."

"You throwing me out of my own house?" I asked, leaning on the door frame.

"You're damn right I am, and until I figure out where I'm going to live. And if you need anything out of here, I suggest you take it with you tonight and that includes your henchman downstairs," she insisted. "And if he's going to be around here, then you better make sure he's told to stay downstairs."

"Like I said, we'll talk about this later," I stood to leave.

"Oh you think I'm bullshitting?!" Medina stood up out the tub. "A dead man has been left on the floor of my house, the only thing I worked hard to own and of value to me, and now you're going to stand there talking to me like walking away is that simple. I don't want to see you or you messing with my head, please just leave."

"Okay," I said, and walked out.

I left Jesse with instructions not to bother Medina and not to go up the stairs. If I could have stayed, I don't think it would have done either of us any good. I was the person Medina needed to hate and my presence only fueled her anger. Within everyone there is a higher and lower self. It's easy to embrace our higher self as opposed to looking into a mirror and coming face to face with the evils we think we're not capable of performing, and Medina was blaming me for her having to release her natural lower nature for survival.

Chapter 24

LEAVING MEDINA WITH JESSE WAS MY FIRST CHOICE because Jesse was more of a family man than street oriented. He was one of those guys that if you didn't look twice, you wouldn't know he was in the room, but if Medina needed someone to talk to, he wasn't too nerdy nor to streetwise.

On my way to the Brotherhood, every exit was telling me to come up off the highway and help Medina process what she was dealing with. Having to kill a man was going to stay with her forever. But if I allowed the Rakehell's rampage to go unchecked, there was no telling who they would go after next. If I didn't take matters in my hands, one of the other families would and there would be no way for me to say when enough is enough.

I pulled into the Brotherhood's parking lot, got out and felt like I was repeating the same steps dealing with the Rakehell problem. It was rare to see all the Lion family in one place gathered in one room. It was never an easy call because a raid of this magnitude would threaten the entire operation. I walked inside the club knowing we had a limited time to take care of business, seeing that the club would be open in a few hours. The looks on everyone's face reflected what they knew, it was about to get ugly and extremely uncomfortable for a lot of people.

"You know why you're here," I started. "Blast is dead." Those words ignited rage and sorrow throughout the club. "It's been a long time since any of us had to be buried or have had to get dirt under our nails. Every line has been crossed by the Rakehells, including an assault on a civilian. My house was violated and my woman was nearly raped and killed tonight!"

The commotion forced me to pause.

"Fuck that, give us the order!" was yelled, and that caused more agitation in the room.

"Oh, you have the order! When you walk out of here, I want this city to be brought to its knees through the chain of command. I'm only stressing that because I don't want to have to deliver the news to your family that I had to deliver to Blast's sister." I went inside my shirt and pulled out my platinum chain and let it dangle.

"You've seen this ring before," I said. "But it was on the finger of Mr. Valentino. I was called to a meeting and this ring was given to me by Mr. Valentino as a merger of the two families." The room erupted. "I wanted to bring this to the table under different circumstances, but we play the cards we are dealt. If I put this ring on, you're looking at the first Black Don this country has ever seen."

"Put it on!" the room yelled.

"I will, but you must know that greater organizational structure and larger responsibilities come with taking over more states, and this Rakehell business will be our first test to show that we can control the streets."

I looked the room over, beyond the shouts and approval, because it was discipline I was looking for. "Right up the street is the Cotton Club, owned by the Italians, and this ring will get us a seat at the table, but this job must not point to the Brotherhood."

The Crazy-Eight's security detail got up and headed towards the door. Their team leader, Major, gave me a nod as he passed me. I pointed at them leaving. "We're done talking," and followed them out of the club.

❦

Castro followed me out of the club to my car.

"I thought they were on the cleanup."

"They were."

"How are they in two places at the same time?"

"I don't question those crazy motherfuckers' tactics. Now their morals are a different thing," he said. "Now if you want me to go, ask them."

"Naw, like you said. I'm sure they have it covered."

"How's Medina taking this?"

"Not good, threw me out the house."

"Whose house, yours?"

"Something like that."

Castro laughed and shook his head from side to side. "Did

she throw you out or are you using that as an excuse to be out here in the mix?" he asked, cutting his eyes over at the Major and his team.

"This has to be done clean, no drive-by shootings with kids being hit by stray bullets making the news."

"Get some fucking sleep, Lion," he said. "You scare me when you're riding on pure adrenaline." He walked off yelling, "And you ain't ever seen my shit on the news!"

I knew the Major was waiting on him to leave. They both avoided each other as much as possible and if it wasn't for me, they would be more enemies than allies.

"Major, how are you, my man?" We shook hands.

"Keys back in the box," he said.

"We tracked the Rakehells to a location in Inkster, you and your team up for another job?"

"All I need is a target and location," he said, fully masked due to Covid and the mirror glasses concealed any signs of life behind his words.

"Look for the GPS coming to you from Castro."

"Just keep your street mobsters out of my cross hairs."

"Don't worry Major," I said, looking over my shoulder and his crew of seven, "But I don't want any of that bullshit you pulled by giving chase that cost me a street mobster."

"Following orders keep us alive, and not following orders cost your mobster his life," the Major shot back as we both climbed into our separate vehicles.

He was a military veteran, and everything to him was about following protocol, which he'd contended street mobsters lacked.

I got back in my car feeling the weight of my eyes closing on me. Castro had suggested I got some rest and I needed it. But I had to make another stop to tie up some loose ends before I could call it a night.

Chapter 25

"HELLO," THE VOICE OF THE TOKYO TWINS CAME through the speakers of my car as I was on I-94 Highway heading to meet up with them.

"Hey, this is Lion."

"Well, hello Mr. Lion," the twin said. "This is Nin, I was hoping you would call me first."

"Okay, well I was heading in your direction and wanted to know if this is a good time for me to drop by. If not, maybe tomorrow we can hook up if this is a bad time," I said due to the loud background noise that sounded like a party was taking place.

"No please," Nin said quickly. "I have to talk to you and we can meet down the hall if you'd like a more private setting."

"Sounds good, I won't take up too much of your time."

"Great, I'll see you soon."

"Alright," I hung up.

That call backfired on me. I was calling to get an update and just suggested I was in the neighborhood with hopes I could get a briefing and headed home. Instead, I set myself up for a meeting.

By the time I pulled inside the parking lot of the Tokyo Twins' condo, I wasn't feeling as antisocial as I did before coming up off the highway. Je'Niece came to my mind, and I laughed at myself thinking maybe I had been living in an illusion thinking I could make a life with someone like Medina. She had her shit together the day we met, and my money didn't move her. She was as opposed to my lifestyle as man was from living on the moon. The thrill of capturing a woman like Medina for me was equal to a hotdog versus a steak dinner.

I got out of my car thinking how both Je'Niece and Ferrell knew what I represented and accepted me for what I did for a living, but Medina wanted nothing to do with the city life, drugs, or the life I had embraced. Now she had been sucked in a dark tunnel.

The buzzer went off before I could push it, and I pulled the door open and stepped inside the corridor heading for the twins' condo. She was holding the door open by the time I got to it.

"Hi," she said, with a sexy smile.

"Looks like date night."

"Not really," she said, closing the door and locking it. "Can I hang your coat for you?"

"Thank you."

"You're welcome." She took my coat, hung it in the closet and turned to catch me admiring her figure.

"You look tense."

"Yeah, it's been a long day."

"Maybe I can help you unwind."

"What does that mean?"

"Well, it depends on if you're here for just business or personal."

"All business is personal, but you know that."

"But personal can be pleasure or profit."

"That's true."

"Please have a seat," Nin said. "I am curious to know if we should have any concerns about the Valentino woman."

"What do you mean?"

"I'll say this to you, if this Ferrell Valentino does not turn out to be who she says she is and if she brings harm to you in any way, I want your permission to be the one to remove her from the table."

"You know I am very close to Mr. Valentino, and he asked me to bring the First Lady up to speed on all the players at the table."

"I understand," Nin said.

"Do you really, because we're talking about a boss of bosses. Ferrell is untouchable by you, and I do not have the power to give you permission to do anything to her, not to mention I am committed to making sure nothing happens to her. And to make myself perfectly clear, Ferrell has enough juice to have all of us wiped out, and I surmise she is going to become aware of her power very fast if she doesn't already know it. With that said, tell me you have something on the Rakehells."

"About the Rakehells," Nin said, "I think we can end this mess within the next several hours. That is if your people are prepared to move on short notice."

"They're on standby."

"Good because sometime before sunrise, we should be receiving a call that Cordelia and her vandals are heading for Inkster. Once that is confirmed, then we should be there to meet them head on."

"Then I better get up out of here because I need to catch a few hours of sleep before things are set in motion."

"Well, since you'll be waiting on the call from us why don't you take my bed, that way you'll be right here when the call comes in."

"That sounds like a good idea but I don't want to put you out of your bed."

"Actually it would be an honor to have you as my guest."

"You sure you don't mind?"

"I'm positive, Lion."

"Then I'll stay".

"Wonderful," Nin said, standing up. "You just relax and I'll change the linen for you."

"Thank you."

"You're very welcome," she said. "This won't take long."

I leaned back on the sofa as Nin dashed out of the room, pulled out my iPhone to check my messages and make a few calls.

"Yeah," Castro said, sounding like I had woke him from his sleep.

"Hope your catnap prepared you to get busy."

"Now?"

"In a few hours I'll give you a call."

"I'll be ready, but I ain't gonna be worth shit if you don't let me catch a couple hours and I suggest you do the same thing."

"The covers are being changed as we speak. I just need you to tell me by the time my feet hit the floor everyone will have been called."

"I'm on it man, that's what I do."

"I'm leaving Major a text, so you don't have to hit him up."

"Bet."

"Alright, till then and Castro."

"I know stay safe, and you do the same."

"Bet," I said and disconnected.

It was time to settle business and put this thing behind us. Bloodshed always interfere with making money, and if pursued too far, it becomes more important than making money. For that reason, it should be avoided at all cost if necessary.

I pressed the button to SEND MESSAGE.

READ. . .

Which told me Major had received and read my text.

It never eased my mind having to call upon Major, and as a matter of fact it made me angry because some people you can call upon to negotiate when calmer heads need to prevail. Then there's men like Major, you only call when negotiations broke down and only one solution remains — to release the war dogs from hell, step back and watch the carnage.

First, I had to get some sleep, and headed for Nin's bedroom.

Chapter 26

THE MOST EFFECT SPELL A WOMEN CAST FROM HER soul is expressed by the details she puts into decorating her bedroom. The entrance to her dwelling acts as a spider's web by drawing bait in closer to its center; a trap most men cannot extricate themselves from once lured into her net.

Nin's bedroom had a highly polished sectional, where the wood floor changed dimension to signal the depth of her web. The entrance into the bedroom was a clean polished light Alaskan pine wood that changed into the light oak, matching the cabinet that held the 55" Smart TV, that stood on a stand and a dresser. Immediately off to the left, where the king size bed was positioned, the floor was crisscrossed dark brown wood, and it was a smoke-stained varnish brown to match the dresser and cabinets.

"I just got it done," Nin said, holding the linen she had taken off the bed in her arms.

"Looks comfortable," I responded, fully inside the bedroom

and seeing the vanity section that held all of Nin's make-up, perfumes, and jewelry. The vanity was about the size of a slender full-length desk and expanded the full length of the bed and the entire mirrored wall. My best guess was the mirror was installed so she could look at herself while having sex with her partner.

"It better be for the price I paid," she said, responding to my comment about the bed looking comfortable.

"Everything looks new."

"I don't get to sleep here very often."

"So this isn't your palace?"

"Oh no, this is my home away from home."

"I see."

"I couldn't see having so much traffic in and out of my home."

"I have a few myself, so I understand."

"Really?!" She acted surprised. "Great minds think alike."

I didn't say anything.

"Okay, if you need anything I'll be in the living room on the sofa.," she said as she turned to leave the room.

Multiple thoughts ran through my head as I watched Nin heading for the door — my falling out with Medina, the pending war that was sure to erupt within a few hours, and the idea that a bullet could be sitting in a chamber waiting to check me out of life. I stood there in a silent thought for a split-second thinking about everything that brought my life to this space in time — the good, the bad, and the ugly.

"Wait," came out of my mouth before Nin got out the door.

"What is it?" She froze in her tracks with her back to me.

"Bed's big enough for two."

"What about what you said earlier?" she said, clinging onto the linen.

"It's possible I might not be around to challenge you."

"We," she turned to face me, "may not be around to know if I wouldn't submit."

"We?"

"You don't think we're pulling out once the call comes in, do you?"

"I was thinking just that."

"Then I wouldn't be a ride or die bitch now, would I?" Nin said, walking closer to me.

"We never discussed this."

"That's what we're doing right now. Besides you can't move without me."

"How do you figure?"

"The call has to come through me, remember?"

"So this means you're in?"

"As far as being in, I'm down," she said, dropping the linen next to my feet. "I've wanted to undress you the very first time we met."

Nin reached in the back of her neck to untie the ribbon that held the one piece in place, and the loosened ribbon that allowed the silk bodysuit to expose her perky nipples as it slid down her waist to the floor. She stepped out of it wearing nothing beneath it but a red satin thong and began taking off my clothes.

"Then that makes two of us, because I've also wanted to unlace you the first time I saw you in all black." The blood bulging in my veins caused my penis to swell in Nin's hand as she stroked it up and down.

"It's so big," she said, pulling on my shaft, then turning around to climb onto the bed, or so I thought, but Nin bend over and put her knee on the bed, then her other foot planted on the floor, and slid the head of my dick up her inner lips to her core, back up and down her tight pussy lips until she creme herself enough for me to grab her by the hips and she guided me into her wetness.

Before long I had given her every inch of me with full thrust as she climbed her other leg onto the bed and spread her legs apart while I stood on the edge of the king size ramming her from behind. The mirror was providing me a full back and front view as well as Nin, and it definitely was a part of motivating my performance. Watching her breast bouncing to the rhythm caused me to dig deeper into her core as creme ran down her thighs and the wetter she became, the faster I pulled her hips into my thrusting.

"Hooooo Lion!" she finally roared, "that's my spot!" She yelled, clawing at the sheets as if she was trying to pull away from the depths of my penetration. It became a push and pull tug of war until I pulled out of her, flipped her over and climbed on top of her as she backpedaled up the king size bed up to the pillow and pulled me deep inside of her fertile walls.

"Hell yeah," was all I could say to how and Nin began lifting her hips off the bed to meet my demands to conquer her. While digging her nails into the flesh of my back, I could feel the sharpness of her nail as I was about to bust a nut.

"Faster!" she exclaimed. "Fuck me harder Lion! Tame this pussy, you fierce Lion... it's all yours," she said, pushing my head down to her breast. "Bite me," she demanded. I bit her nipple and she screamed, "Mmmuuuu!" until it became almost S&M.

"Oh shit!" Nin yelled. "Take this pussy, it's yours," her words tapering off into a whisper as I released inside of her.

"God damn that was good," I said, then collapsed next to her on the bed.

"It's time," Nina, the other Tokyo Twin said flatly, turned and exits the bedroom. I cannot say how long she had been standing there watching us, but Nin just turned on her stomach.

I sat up on the edge of the bed preparing to get dressed.

"I'll give you whatever you want, but you can't have both of us."

"Come again?"

"You can't fuck both of us," Nin said, still laying on her stomach, then turning on her side to face me.

"Who said anything about fucking your sister?"

"You didn't but she did."

"Is this some twin vibe because I didn't see her standing there let alone say anything," I said. "Besides, I have no intentions of screwing Nina."

"See this mark right here?" Nin said, twisting her hip over and showing me a birthmark on the back of her thigh.

"Yeah, I see."

"This is the only thing that makes us different, so if you aren't sure of which one of us you're about to fuck, then this is will tell you if it's me or my sister."

"I get your point."

"Do you?"

"I think I do."

"All of my life we've shared everything — clothes, ideas, money, power, and yes, men. I just want something I don't have to share and can call my own."

"Look, I can't say after tonight where this will lead, but I give you my word of honor that I'll look for your birth mark before I spread your legs apart."

"That's all I wanted to hear," Nin sat up next to me on side of the bed and smiled. "Even if things don't go as planned on our mission, just hearing you say that makes all the difference in the world."

"Good, now can I go clean myself up and get dressed before she comes back?"

"I'll have to go with you," Nin stood up. "We don't have time to go separately."

The shower we took was quick, but not so quick that we did not have time for some after play. It was not my intention to get into a round of twister with Nin or pinning her up against the wall of the steaming hot shower but trying to move around each other in such a small space created more heat than being between the sheets, and two wet bodies bumping and lathering only led to more heat, pleasure, and desire. There is nothing like exchanging fluids to fuel the quest for power.

Chapter 27

RARE IS IT WE WALK INTO BATTLE WITHOUT THE EXPECTATIONS of not coming out alive on the other side.

"Good morning, Tokyo family," Nin said in her mild voice to a squad of women who were lined up to go to battle.

I wondered if all the women could hear her until they snapped to an attention. It was an impressive display that commanded respect. Bearing in mind that these were women who just a few hours prior all sat around laughing and playing dress up in what could have been considered a pajama party. And not to get it twisted, I was not restraining my smile because I thought their display was cute, but because of their ability to transform from cute to deadly as sin. Nin walked a single filed line in the hallway as I trailed behind her, listening to her instruct these women to not only walk up to death's door, but to enter with grace, honor and be proud of the cause they served.

The women fell out of roll call starting from the far end of the hallway and by the time we stepped outside, where Nina was standing in observance, there was an organized caravan of Range Rover's extending from the front entrance of the condo all the way down the parking lot and pass my Jaguar, which I was heading towards.

"Why don't you take point with me," Nin said before I could leave her side. Only the two of us had stopped, the others jumping in the Rovers four per vehicle.

"Fine," I said, then climbing in the backseat of the door that had been opened for me.

Nin stood next to her driver until she closed my door. By the time she walked around to the passenger's side, a high polished dark skinned woman held Nin's door open until she was seated next to me.

"Listen up, ladies," Nin said. "Because this is the Lion family's operation, I'm going to turn my command over to Lion himself. You are now to listen to him and only answer to him until this project is over."

Nin then handed me an earpiece. She went on giving her final instructions as I placed the earpiece in my ear and placed a call to Castro.

"Yeah," Castro answered his phone.

"What's our status?"

"We're in position."

"Where you at?" I asked.

"The team is headed that way on 94 Freeway."

"Oh, I'm with the Tokyo family heading your way."

"Alright, stay safe."

"Bet, stay safe." I ended the call.

"They're waiting," Nin said, looking over at me and pointing at the earpiece.

"Do I need to do anything for them to hear me?"

"They've been listening to every word you've said."

Without saying a word, I tapped my phone and Nin shook her head up and down, indicating my entire phone call had been heard.

I cleared my throat, adjusted the earpiece and said, "Good morning Tokyo family," as the caravan came off the 94 freeway onto Lenox Township, and parked near a construction site. "Just so I'm comfortable knowing you all can hear me clearly, why don't you flick your headlights once."

The entire line lights came on and went back off. "Very well," I said. "This mission is cut and dry. You don't need a long speech from me because I know you're highly skilled at your trades. Something sacred of ours has been violated and we are called to respond. I stand with this family as I defend my own. The Brotherhood was shot up by the Rakehells, blood was shed, and our only recourse is to send a message to the Rakehells and to the future, that anyone who even thinks of coming at us will be wiped off the face of the map. My instructions are simple: seek and destroy anyone claiming to be or supporting the cause of Rakehell."

Nin touched my arm.

"Let us give them their last mistake in blood."

My adrenaline was running high by the time I pulled the earpiece out of my ear.

"Leave it in," Nin said.

I did as she said, and when I stuck it back into my ear it became apparent why Nin wanted me to leave it in. The women were worked up and the chatter was almost like hearing a thousand bees buzzing after being worked into a frenzy.

"You have their attention," she said with a smile, covering her earpiece with the palm of her hand.

I had not questioned the reason why we had parked on the side of a construction site, and after my call to arms was issued, it all became crystal clear why we were there. The construction site turned out not to be under construction after all. The eighteen-wheeler bed was slung open to reveal heavy artillery. Who would have ever suspended that a cargo full of weapons could be sitting right in plain view with thousands of people riding pass it for days, weeks, and perhaps months because I couldn't say how long the guns had been sitting there. Each vehicle was being loaded as suit of armor, with the women filing out of their cars one by one arming themselves as if this move had been performed many times. That was until the car in front of us was loaded and Nin said, "We're up," opened her door and headed for her weapons of choice.

I got out and followed behind her.

"Well, hello Mr. Lion," the woman in combat gear looking down at me from the eighteen-wheeler said. "I know the weapons of choice for these women, but you look like someone who likes sending a powerful message."

"Let me guess, you're the sergeant-at-arms," I said, looking up at her, and the crates stretching the full length of the cabin.

"Let me guess," the sergeant-at-arms handed down the very

same weapon Tony Montana used in the movie Scarface, two military munitions boxes, and a few extra magazines.

By the time I made it back to the passenger's seat, the car behind us was passing us by to be outfitted for battle, and we sat there until the sergeant-at-arms pulled the cabin door closed and jumped down in one motion, at which point the armed caravan began moving. The chatter that had filled my earpiece was now silent as we got back on the expressway.

"Yeah," I said, answering my phone.

"Where you at?" Castro asked.

"We're about to hit the lodge, where you at?"

"On the lodge."

"Keep me posted," I hung up and touched the back backseat of our driver. "Keep this speed limit to the lodge."

I pressed my earpiece, "Last car pull up to my nine."

Our driver looked through her rearview mirror at me for a second then back at the road.

The rear car pulled up next to us. "Scout two miles ahead of us," I instructed. "Cars two and three stay on car nine's tailgate." Nin looked over into the backseat to see Nina pulling out ahead of us.

They did as instructed and before long, Nina could be overheard saying, "Is that them?"

"Report car nine."

"Oh my lord," Nina said, "The Lion family has taken over the highway."

"Good," I said. "Have the cars caught up to you?"

"Yes, but Castro is directing them to join the other cars," Nina said. "This is bananas."

"This is war," I said.

There was radio silence until we met up with the Lion family and the scouts that accompanied them. The Tokyo family were impressive in their own rights and being on the inside, told me they were formidable opponents to be taken very seriously. If I had doubts about their ability to takeover and maintain control of the Rakehells' areas, it had been suspended as I rode into battle with them. They had sealed my vote at the table as long as the sun stayed to our backs.

Chapter 28

AS THE SUNRISE DAZZLED OVER THE HORIZON ON A cold winter's day, the devil's dance started on the opposite side of its beauty by the sounds of rapid automatic gun fire.

If it had been Mortal Combat or a box office movie, the sound effects with all of its boom, rat-ta-ta-ta-tat, and bullets being spit out by drum clips would have been award winning, even its graphics, but this wasn't the Hollywood life.

Almost immediately after the Rakehells' caravan brake lights was spotted turning off the corner of Palmer Road in Inkster, the high intensity of a gun battle began. Before I could radio for confirmation, roads were being blocked and bullets began flying from every open car door and from windows. They were boxed in.

"Don't give them an ounce of air to breathe!" I yelled, stepping from the backseat and locking a miniature rocket into the mouth of the chamber as I looked for a target to fire upon.

It quickly became evident by the way the Rakehells were

positioning themselves back and forth to close the gaps around the center car, that Madame de Cordelia was caught with her panties down.

"Don't aim for the center car!" I yelled into my earpiece, then turned and yelled out to everyone, "Don't aim for the heart, not yet!"

When I turned back around the Rakehells, car doors were being kicked open and their weapons led the way with heavy sparks ripping from their barrels. Some were using their vehicles as cover while others dove face down in the snowy slush. Soon the smell of gun smoke joined the fresh morning air.

Finally the target I was waiting for appeared at the rear bumper to their left rank. The rocket left the killer weapon like it had jet fuel boosters aiming directly at death. Then the Rakehells went into rear form.

"Pain in the morning!" was yelled from one of the Rakehells.

"Pain in the morning!" was repeated in unison by them all.

They were singing as if in boot camp.

Castro laughed, "Bitches want to go out in style," then emptied an entire clip from his HK, reloaded, and repeated his assault on the singing Rakehells.

"Uhhh!"

"Yeah, ain't no cowards over here!" one of the Rakehells yelled, taking pleasure in knowing his bullet had hit one of our men.

"Keep your fuckin head low," Castro yelled out at our first wounded.

I turned just in time to see it wasn't our man Castro was yelling at, but he was talking to one of the Tokyo women.

"Shit," I said, "I got her." I ducked down and moved over to her position. "Jessica!" I yelled, she was frozen in her tracks.

"Yeah," she answered, looking down at me.

I don't know how she hadn't been riddled with bullets because each time I reached up to grab her, bullets flying past me put me back on my ass.

"I think I'm jammed, can you help me?" I lied, but it worked. She rushed down next to me, "Got it!" I cocked the hammer.

She looked at me with a blank stare. "Are you here to kill or here to die?" I asked her.

No response. "Look at me!" I yelled. "Do you want to die today?"

"No, I don't," she answered.

"Then why are you making yourself an easy target?"

"I was just thinking how crazy it is to be shooting at someone we were partying with a few weeks ago."

"I know, but you got to fight."

"Okay," she said.

"You locked and loaded?"

She checked and nodded up and down.

"Okay, when I stand up I'm going to need for you to cover me long enough for me to get a clean shot."

"I'm scared," she said.

"But your weapon knows no fear, just point and shoot."

"Okay, I got your back."

"I'm out of fuckin' bullets over here!" Nin yelled, pulling out her sidearm and knocking holes in the side door that pierced through and knocked her target into the open. Several guns rocked him off his feet as he fell backwards with his gun still firing off shots that cut through the sky.

Jessica sprung to life either from me talking to her or Nin's yelling. Whichever it was, she snatched the rear door open and pulled out extra clips and rushed them over to Nin, where she knelt down beside Nin and lit the block up as Nin reloaded.

"Now!" I yelled. "Aim for the center car!"

My miniature rocket lifted the backend of the car three off the ground and bounced back to earth. Everyone took aim at the car with the Rakehells trying with all of their manpower to ward off the assault and taking one casualty after another as their numbers dwindled just as hard as my banana clips hit the ground. As far as I could tell, at least one of the Crazy-Eight who had mad sniper skills had taken position resting his rifle between the frame of an open door and whoever he was aiming at wasn't going to live to tell the story.

The target was in sight and we were basically climbing over each other to pick off those who were still clinging to life.

"Start drawing your team down," I told Nin.

"What?!" she responded. "Not until we finished what we came here for."

"It won't take all of us to finish them off."

I had turned command of the Tokyo family back over to Nin with the same instructions being given to Castro to draw down and have the Lion family start pulling back. I sat with my back up against the car we came in, watching carloads of both families leaving a bloody massacre.

The few that remained began closing in on Madame

Cordelia's battered Rolls-Royce. Nin and the Crazy-Eight followed a tight formation, each of us careful not to walk upon a wounded Rakehell with a live weapon in their hand, and kicking them away from their dead bodies.

Switch, the Crazy-Eight's bomb tech placed a timer explosive on the Rolls-Royce as we all took cover behind the mangled wreckage.

"How can we be sure she's in there if he's going to blow the car to hell?" Nin asked.

"Just be ready to take your shot."

Nin loaded her M16, then put it over her shoulder and took out a 44 Magnum, locking it in the grips with both hands just as Switch ran behind one of the abandoned cars for cover. Everyone ducked out of sight until the explosion released an earth-shaking eruption.

Madame Cordelia's driver was the first to appear from the mangled classic vehicle. He stumbled out from behind the steering wheel dazed and confused, rocked by the explosion, and looking as if he didn't know where he was. Steadying himself as best he could, he folded over and coughed harshly before standing upright and throwing his hands in the air.

"Wait!" he surrendered.

"Is she there?" Nin asked, leveling her weapon at him.

"I'm just her driver," he appealed.

"I'll take that as a yes," she said and put four rounds in his chest and one between his eyes. He took one painful gasp of air and went down like a dead weight, and still there was no sign of Madame Cordelia.

Switch ran up to the driver's door and threw a teargas canister inside, closed the door shut and ran for cover. The wait was not long until the back door swung open forcing the teargas and Madame Cordelia out of the car, on her hands and knees. She crawled away from the gas chamber of a car. Cordelia's hair was unkept, clothes dangled loosely from her body as if all the shots aimed at the car took direct effect on her.

"Make this quick!" I said to Nin, looking around to make sure no one was left alive.

"Stand up you basic ass bitch," Nin said and moved in for a personal shot.

"What's wrong, Nin?" Cordelia spoke. "You can stab me in the back but can't shoot a lady while I'm down?"

"You're just lucky I don't have time to dismember you limb by limb."

"If you're looking for an apology when I know you're going to kill me anyway, then you might as well get it over with."

"This isn't a death you can talk your way out of," Nin said, pulling the M16 from her shoulder and riddled Madame Cordelia with bullets, and did not stop despite Cordelia's body hitting the pavement. She walked over and stood atop her, emptied the clip into her, then dropped the weapon next to her head.

"She had that clip coming to her the moment I knew she was going to be trouble," Nin said, getting in the car.

Only the Crazy-Eight stayed behind, and jumped in their rides leaving behind their hallmark trade as guns for hire.

Chapter 29

96 FREEWAY. "SO, WHAT ARE YOU GOING TO DO NOW that all of this is behind us?" Nin asked.

"You think this is behind us?"

"Isn't it?" Nin questioned. "They're all dead."

We had changed cars and was riding in a Hummer.

"How many families did we reject last month that wanted a seat at the Brotherhood's table?"

"I think it was three under consideration and six denials."

"And that was in one month."

"Yeah, so what's your point?"

"My point is as long as there are families knocking on our door wanting a piece of the American dream, it will always have to be defended."

"Oh, I can see that."

"The real question is, how far are you willing to go to maintain your piece of the city?"

"I never looked at it that way."

"Maybe you should start."

"I will."

Changing the subject wasn't a way of denying the lives lost behind us, it was a part of the business we were in and was just another day at the office.

"Ever think about giving this lifestyle up?" Nin asked, looking at the traffic.

"Who doesn't?"

"What else would you do?"

"I made my choices, this is what I do."

The ride with Nin was helping me decide on putting on the Legion family ring. I wasn't thinking of a different lifestyle or a way out. I was digging myself in deeper into the one I was living.

"Maybe you should start giving it some thought," Nin said.

"What about you," I said to get the subject off me. "How long do you plan to languish in this life style?"

"I have an off ramp."

"So you're ready to throw in the towel?"

"I don't see it that way."

"Then how do you see it?"

"My sister and I came into this with a projected goal and once that goal is reached, then this way of life will have ran its course."

"I need to hang out with you more often to pick your brain," I said, pulling into the condominiums where Nin lived and next to my Jaguar.

"If you come visit, then maybe I'll give you some investment tips."

"I'll keep that in mind," I said, stepping out of the Hummer.

"Thank you for being so kind to me."

"The pleasure was mutual I'm sure."

"Bye Lion."

"See you later, Nin."

Good conversations always leave you something to think about or open your mind to seeing things from a different perspective.

Chapter 30

THE BEST CHESS MOVE IS PLANNING SO FAR AHEAD OF your opponent until you can see checkmate six or eight moves before you move your first pawn. Nothing can stand in a man or woman's way when you're thinking of your options as opposed to feeling trapped into making one forced decision.

Everything that I had going for me was gained because I believed that living on the edge of life, and not playing the hand dealt to me at a safe distance was the only way to change my conditions. I was heading down the 94 Expressway and had closed the chapter on the Rakehells. But not entirely, what I didn't tell Nin was why once blood is shed on the streets it isn't over that simply. The family business had been taken care of but that did not mean the old man would be pleased with the outcome. My power only ran so far up the chain, which meant in order to rise to the top, it had to be done with the least amount of blood spilled.

I had the ring, an opportunity that would never come around

a second time. I had rolled the dice and it was finally paying off, but it also meant stepping deeper into a world that had no exit ramp that Nin spoke of having. She was still small enough in the game to be able to walk away and could easily be replaced. I had to admit the feelings inside of me was as raw as being the king of the jungle could get. I had gone into battle and came out with the power of the lives that were taken, and if the power in my possession was challenged up the road, I was fully equipped and prepared to put them also in that mirror. Nin's questions made me think about Medina, who wanted a life for me that I wasn't sure I wanted or deserved.

I had a criminal mind with so many codes of life and had broken so many laws until morals had become the least of my concerns. The Rakehells had made the fatal miscalculation of thinking they could cheat the rules of the Brotherhood and believing if they stood their ground, above all things.

Chapter
31

BEYOND SACRIFICE LIES REWARD. BY THE TIME I pulled up to the entrance gate of the Valentino's mansion and opened the gate, the phone call between Castro and I had ended. Everyone had made it safely back to the city, and with the exception of a few bullet grazes and jagged nerves, no one needed medical attention, nor did I have to visit any families to deliver bad news.

The gate as it turned out was on a timer, once opened it closed automatically. I can't say why I chose to go to Ferrell's place, it's just where my thoughts took me.

Once inside, I did not know what to do next. The keys were mine, the gate opener was mine, but inside I was lost. Perhaps it was the furniture, which was dated, and I decided right there once Ferrell got back, we'd do some furniture shopping. Of all the rooms, the only one that did meet my standard of taste was Ferrell's bedroom, it was plush, and everything was young as far as style went.

Mr. Valentino did me a favor and took everything from his bedroom with him. It was the only empty room in the mansion, except for a single nightstand he left behind. It would be the room I'd set up for myself, I thought as I pulled the door open and returned to Ferrell's bedroom.

I took my clothes off and laid them on the chair next to the nightstand and looked out of the window for a long time staring at the golf course wearing only my boxer briefs. The golf course was the greenest of green even during the winter months. Snow patches were here and there, with leafless trees sloped to the side, but what made the sight so peaceful is there was no movement as far as the eyes could see, or maybe it was because it was the first time in a long time that my thoughts could slow down. I stood there in that one spot until I felt my body began to calm itself and my limbs relaxed from the tension of the street battle.

I went and took a shower, then climbed butt naked in Ferrell's bed, got back up, drew the drapes closed and climbed back under the covers.

⌒✕✕✕⌒

Nightfall had blanketed the golf course by the time I had awakened. The LED lights lit the course like a painting you would see hanging on the walls of a vacation advertisement planner's office. I had built up an appetite from the desperately needed sleep and decided to go downstairs to get something to eat, which I did wearing only my boxer briefs and the chain around my neck that I placed the Valentino's ring on. It was where Andrew kept it before giving it to me, so I thought it was a good place to start.

There wasn't anything to be considered junk food or a quick bite to eat in the kitchen, except for some fruit, so I grabbed a green apple and continued looking the interior over room by room. The parlor had to be an Italian design; everything was old fashioned like you'd see in the Godfather movies. Even the phone, which scared the hell out of me when it rung, had an old fashioned ringer and had a loud ring to it. I stood there for a second thinking maybe I should just let it ring until the caller gave up, but curiosity got the best of me.

"Hello," I said, and almost said, "Valentino residence."

"You're there," the unknown voice said, but spoke as if he knew me.

"Yeah I'm here," I said. "Who are you?" I said and looked for some place to throw the apple away.

"We've been trying to reach you, Mr. Lion," the caller ignored my question.

"Yeah, well you got me so why don't you tell me who's been looking for me?" All of a sudden I felt like I was caught with my underwear down.

He laughed, "It's me Lion, David."

"Mr. Valentino's David?"

"I guess you can say that."

My blood began to boil at the thought of David playing with me and not immediately revealing it was him, who sounded nothing like he did in person.

"Well, what can I do for you David?" I asked.

"Nothing."

"Nothing, then why are you calling me?"

"Well, Mr. Lion your absence seems to have an impact on Ferrell. She is the reason I'm calling."

"Is she okay?"

"Quite fine I would say."

"Then why didn't she call me herself? She has my number."

"You'll have to ask her that question yourself, Mr. Lion," David said. "I only do what I'm asked to do."

And did they tell you to call here playing games? I started to ask but kept it to myself.

"Are you still there?" the lackey David asked.

"I'm here, where's Ferrell?"

"Oh, she's around here someplace."

"And just where is someplace, David?"

I sat down in the chair next to the coffee table that held the phone.

"Well this estate is quite large, so I'll just have to find her and let her know we talked."

"I thought you said she had you to find me."

"She did."

"Look man," I said. "Either you're confused or trying to confuse me. Either way, I don't have time for no fuckin' games."

I had lost it with this prick and all of his casual mumbo jumbo talk. Dude was kicking it like we were buddies catching up on old times and somehow, I would enjoy talking to him longer than to deliver the message and keep it moving.

"Okay fine," David said, somewhat snipped. "By now you know how I feel about your type."

"My type?" "Yeah, your type, that's right."

"What does my type mean?"

"Never mind all of that, I was told to do whatever to find you," David snapped at me. "I was told to be nice when we spoke, that's all I was trying to do but since you called me out, then it's not my fault things fell off track."

"First off, me and you don't come from the same tracks! Just tell me what you called to tell me become I really don't give a sweet fuck about establishing a cordial friendship with you!"

David paused, "Your presence is required up state."

"What, is that supposed to mean something to me?"

"Your flight plans have been made and you should not keep the table waiting."

I sat up in my chair, "You lost me with your boy scout talk, so why don't you start again?"

He took a deep breath into the phone. "The Valentinos want you in Massachusetts, Mr. Lion."

"Ferrell's back in the States?"

"Yes."

"Why didn't you just say that then, man?"

"I just did."

"Where's Mr. Valentino?"

"He's here as well."

"Then why don't you put one of them on the phone?"

"I told you this place is—""If you think I'm going to hop on a plane for someplace I've never been on your word, then you're insane."

"Then you'll just have to stay on the line while I find them."

Before I could say anything the phone was roughly put down, at which point I got up and began pacing the floor until the cord stop me in my tracks. So, I paced back and forth as far as the cord would stretch while I waited for someone to get on the phone and explain to me why David was trying to get me on a plane to Massachusetts. As far as I was concerned, it could have been a hit placed on my head and to get me as far away from Michigan as possible to never be found alive. For David's sake, Andrew or Ferrell needed to pick up the phone or I was going to hunt him down and feed him to the forest as fertilizer. David had lost his position because of Mr. Valentino's unwillingness to trust him to wear the family ring and he blamed me for getting in his way of becoming the next boss of bosses, and that in my opinion was worth flying a man across the country to be killed. Nice try, wrong guy because I'm not a goddamn fool.

However, if things were on that level, getting out of Michigan for a minute was appealing considering the events that had occurred with the Rakehell bloodshed. But that too, presented a situation because maybe the bosses thought I made too much noise and needed to shut me down. You just never know who you've ticked off at the round table until the lights are turned on, and the closer I got to the top, the more attention they paid to my actions. But if I was going to be taken out, it wasn't going to be by the likes of David.

"Lion," Ferrell voice answered the phone.

I smiled and sat back down in the chair. "Wassup stranger."

She laughed, "I'm fine Mr. Lion."

"When did you get back?"

"You would know if you bothered to answer your phone. I've been calling and calling you."

"Sorry about that, but you know how it is."

"No, I don't, Lion. But I want to know how it is. And I want to tell you something."

"Yeah and what's that?"

"No, not over the phone. Did David tell you the family wants to meet?"

"He told me,"

"Oh, my God! What did you say to him? He was pale when he told me you were on the phone. Did you two have it out?"

I sat there smiling, joyful inside to be talking to Ferrell and even more joyful at the thought that I had gotten under David's skin.

"We exchanged a few words," I said.

"Oh, Lion. Please try to be nice to him. He's been with us for a long time, and you know his feelings have been hurt by this whole thing."

I wanted to tell her if she had not answered the phone, I was going to be real nice to David whenever I saw him again by beating his ass a few times.

"I'll try," I said instead.

"Please do it for me."

"Let me get going, I need to pack."

"That won't be necessary. I've picked some things up for you."

"Really?"

"Yes, they have a different style here and you need to blend in and not be the flamboyant type."

"Damn, I thought my style—""It's perfect for Detroit, and you represent it well, but I want to see you in silk Italian suits as well."

Maybe I should have shown a little more interest in what Ferrell wanted to tell me to encourage her into expressing herself. Whatever it was that had caused her reluctance to speak over the phone had piqued my interest. And because she had decided to put off telling whatever it was she wanted to tell me, it made me a little more nervous. I wasted no time preparing myself to leave the mansion and head up to the estate. On second thought, I was never very high on surprises, and putting anything off until later also fit in that category.

Chapter 32

THE AERION SUPERSONIC BUSINESS JET, AS I WAS TOLD
before boarding the jet by its pilot, could cruise at Mach 1.6 and
whiz from Michigan to Paris in about four hours — more than
three hours faster than a Gulfstream V. The Aerion jet's straight
wings reduced drag and afforded the aircraft the ability to slip
through the air like a hot butter knife cutting through butter.

He could have saved the aviator glasses talk and just told me he
was about to pin my ass to the chair getting me to Massachusetts
— and was reached much faster than I had imagined possible.

Ascending the jet stairs was the same scene as it was leaving
the Michigan airport. Italians in expensive suits positioned
themselves to meet my arrival, or the jet itself, only this time
there were two faces there that I knew. David was standing at
the front end of the car smoking a cigarette and Ferrell was being
let out of the backseat by the limousine driver.

A red carpet ran from the steps straight to the limousine, and

Ferrell stepped onto it and headed towards me with a big smile forming on her face.

"Hey handsome," she said with her arms held out to greet me, and kissed both sides of my cheeks before hugging me.

"Hey First Lady," I returned with a hug.

"How was your flight?" she asked, taking my arm as we walked to the car.

"Fast."

"Wow! I know, right?"

David butted the cigarette and approached me. I gave him half of a head nod, not as a greeting but more of a 'some other time and another place we were going to finish our last conversation'.

"Oh, you two," Ferrell said, knowing the tension between us, before climbing into the back of the limo.

I looked at David and nodded a gesture for him to go first getting inside.

"Three's a crowd," he said, looking inside at Ferrell. "I'll be riding with Mikey." He looked at me and walked away.

I climbed inside, and the driver shut the door. Seconds later, we were on the move.

"Oh my God," Ferrell said. "Where's the ring, Lion?"

"I have it."

"You have it where?"

"On my chain."

Ferrell went inside my shirt and began looking for the clamp to take the chain from my neck.

"This isn't Detroit, Michigan Lion." She took the chain from around my neck, "You're not in a position to walk in here and throw your weight around. Here, put it on."

"I thought we had this discussion already."

"We did but this is different."

"Different how?" I asked without talking the ring from her hand.

"If you walk in there without this ring on your finger, they will be offended. Why do you think David is acting the way he is?"

"What, what does David have to do with me not wearing that ring? He wants to put it on and that's why he's acting the way he's acting."

"Lion, this is not about David."

"Then why did you bring him up?"

"Lion please, I told them you accepted Andrew's offer and he has assured them you accepted, so please put the ring on before we get out of this car."

"If I put this ring on then it stays on," I took the ring from her hand.

"Lion, spare me the antics of your ego, and put the ring on."

"Okay, I don't want to put Andrew on the spot."

"It isn't Andrew you would be putting on the spot," Ferrell said. "He's out and I'm the boss now."

"Then I certainly don't want to put you on the spot," I said, sliding the ring on my figure.

Ferrell looked at the ring on my finger. "Your other finger, baby."

"You want me to take off my ring?"

"No, put the ring on your pinky finger."

I did as she said and we both looked at the perfect fit. The rest of the ride was pretty much in silence. I, for one, was thinking about where this road would take me, and Ferrell seemed be taking in the scenery as well as being consumed by her own thoughts.

"We're here," she said.

"Here where, all of this?" I asked, which was so much property all I saw was land until we got into the clearing, and still the house sat back far on the property with nothing but a forest as the front yard. The property was isolated away from the rest of the world. "I got you here, but I can't speak for you, Lion. I'm sure they will like you as much as Andrew and I like you," she said as the limo pulled alongside the other vehicles that appeared to be under the watchful eyes of the guards.

"Let's hope so," I said.

"You'll do fine."

For the first time, butterflies began dancing in my stomach as we got closer to the massive sized home. Security appeared to be all over the estate, standing around cars, in booths, peering out of windows, on the roof tops, and walking K9's through the forest on long leashes. It was worlds apart from the city streets I came from.

The limousine driver opened our door, and all eyes were on us when we stepped out of the limo. David, along with three other Italians stood close by to escort us inside.

"Everyone is preparing for the meeting," Ferrell said, "so you might want to try to get some rest, and I can't say what time the Commission will send for you."

It was the first time Ferrell used the word "Commission".

"Will you be present?" I asked as we stepped inside the house.

"Yes, I have a seat at the table."

The three guards that escorted us in the house did not come in with us and were replaced by two others once we were inside, accompanied by an elderly butler that carried heavy bags beneath his eyes which I noticed by how wide-eyed he looked at me. He took point moving swiftly for his age and made up for it by his lack of words, using mostly hand gestures to keep up, staying quiet as he passed certain doors, and motioning us down the hallway that had guards sitting by closed doors, all except one door that was open. I stole a glance as we walked past and saw that it was occupied by an elderly gentleman and a very young nurse in uniform standing over him appearing to have been injecting the man with something. Guards stood by watching her and they barely glanced up at us walking past the room.

"You'll be sleeping here," Ferrell said, touching the butler on his shoulder as he opened the door and left without a word. "If you need anything, just have one of the guards get Ralph for you," she said, stepping inside of the bedroom ahead of me.

"Where are you staying?" I asked, noticing David stayed in the hallway.

"I'll be down the hall," she responded. "Are you nervous?"

"Not at all, why you ask me that?"

She laughed, "Okay tough guy."

"Yeah, where's my watch?" I asked to change the subject.

"With my luggage."

My phone rang. "Lion," I said.

"I thought you were going to check in when you got there," Castro said.

"I just got here, what's up?"

"Got some bad news, man."

"So bad it can't wait until I get back?" I looked at Ferrell.

"Do you want me to leave?" she asked, more hand gesturing than verbally.

I put one finger in the air as a sign not to leave.

"It's Pharaoh, man."

"What about him?"

"I think ah, he's gone."

"Gone? . . . What do you mean gone?"

Castro let out a sigh, "I'm not sure, but I think he's dead—""You calling me on an assumption?"

"Nah."

"Then is he dead or not, Castro?"

I had to ask the question, but did not want to know the answer as I watched Ferrell cover her mouth.

"Yeah, he's dead Lion. I'm sorry man."

"Where is he?" I asked, then sat down at the foot of the bed, turning my back on Ferrell.

"This the thing man. He was taken to the hospital last night. He was in bad shape off that but alive."

"Castro! . . . Castro, stop."

We both were silent for a minute.

"Now tell me the real—" I finally said after my head stop spinning.

"Word is someone shot some drugs in his I.V. bag."

"Someone shot dope in his I.V. bag?"

"But we on it, dawg. A few of Pharaoh's junkie friends were with him so we are thinking one of them did it."

"Don't do nothing until I get back there, you got it? Nothing?!""I hear you man, but there's something else."

"I'm listening."

"Someone from your fam was there as well."

"Open the basement for interrogation."

"You want the Crazy-Eight's hand in on this?"

"Maybe not," I said. "Just put your ear to the streets."

"Sorry to be the messenger of bad news."

"When I get back, I don't want anyone knowing I'm back."

"Got it."

I hung up the phone distraught.

"I have to get back to Detroit," I told Ferrell.

"What's happened?"

"Pharaoh's dead."

"Oh no, I'm so sorry to hear that Lion."

"I'm going to need you to apologize to the families for my absence."

Ferrell closed the door and came to sit next to me, and I swear I saw a grin on David's face before she closed the door.

"I know that this is terrible news for you Lion, and I apologize for your loss, but you above all people know the price for failing to appear before the Commission and their decisions are final."

"You can speak for me or Andrew can talk to them on my behalf."

"He's dead, Lion," she said firmly. "What can you do for him in four hours that can't be done in twelve hours?"

"If this was Andrew—""But it's not!" She stood up from beside me and looked down at me. "And if it was Andrew, I'd like to think you wouldn't allow me to do anything out of character."

"Out of character?"

"Yes, because if this were a meeting called by the Brotherhood, you would fine or oust someone for their failure to appear."

I had no retort, as I watched Ferrell turn to leave the room. "I'll give you some privacy to grieve and weigh your options," she said and closed the door behind her, leaving the strongest point she made, that there was nothing flying back to Michigan could accomplish. Dead is dead and that's a finality that could not be reversed even if I skipped out on the Commission and offended everyone here. It sounded logical but did nothing for the walls building up inside of me.

As odd as it seemed, I sat there questioning whether I had a right to feel hurt by Pharaoh's death. Here, in less than twenty-four hours, I had been responsible for killing and ordering the deaths of more people than I cared to remember and felt nothing for the grief I had caused their families and had not even given it much thought until that moment. The Rakehells may have been terrible drug dealers, but they had families who would have to bury their bullet riddled bodies. Some would say that I had only reaped what I had sown by the blood that was on my hands of which I could identify with in a strange way. It was that thought that caused me to hold back the tears that built up in my eyes. I refused to grieve not because I was not hurting inside but because somehow, I felt I had no right to feel what others felt due to my lifestyle decisions. For a brief moment, I felt as if the many souls I had taken were hovering over me waiting to see a tear roll down my face, and out of sheer rebellion for those who I knew wanted to see me suffering, both in and after life, I stamped down my pain just for the spite of it. If Pharaoh's death was being used to measure my ability to lead the Lion family or intended to break my resolve, then I hoped there were tears in the afterlife because in this one I was only out to extract tears of pain from those who brought it upon themselves by crossing me the wrong way. Truth be told, there are only two kinds of people in a democracy — victims and those who take advantage of the victims. I was not a victim, nor would I be reduced to being one in this lifetime. Tears were the result of pain overwhelming those who had felt somehow victimized by the powers above, whether you call it God, government, life, death, or destiny.

I had a date with my destiny, a Commission that could give everything I've worked for meaning, and Pharaoh had met his in the form of a needle. I had done my part to ease his suffering, something no one else had known about. So, I should not have felt guilty for supplying him with the drugs to support his habit. The doctors diagnosed him with cancer, and because he had no insurance, the medical industry turned its back on him and kicked him out on the streets to self-medicate his pain away.

Ferrell was right, nothing could be accomplished in four hours that couldn't be done in twelve, and since death doesn't take a vacation, neither should I. Going before the committee would benefit Ferrell but for me it would empower the Lion family beyond measure. I ran the streets, but I didn't own any political leaders, no judges were in my pocket, nor did I control the outcome on the future. Money was just a tool to get those things, power moved the money to make change. I had the money, power on the streets, and with the Commission's blessing, the Valentino's ring would get the Lion family the respect we deserved.

Chapter
33

THE COMMISSION GOT ON ITS WAY AND RAN INTO THE lunch hour. Ralph, the butler brought me breakfast and later lunch to my room. I came to find out I was not the only one there who had to go before the Commission. Men and women had been flown in from all over the globe to either cast a vote or be seen. It wasn't a Commission set alone to establish made men, but also consisted of those going before the committee for violating certain codes of conduct, dues, and the making of judges, which I thought was done by the justice system. Wrong. People are made in the shadows long before they're made in public. As it turned out, Ralph was a bit of a talker when he discovered why I was there and had no problem reporting back to me between meals who was made and who got the ax. It was his opinion that I was being saved for last because I had a shoo-in by having the Valentino girl, as he called her, sponsor me, and held Andrew Valentino in high regard. He said no person the

Legion had ever brought before the Commission had ever been vetoed by another family.

Ferrell was part of the body now and had to sit in on the hearings. She could not come see me but every opportunity she found time to whisper a few words to Ralph, he wasted no time delivering the message.

I had been moved from the loss of Pharaoh. I went from being frustrated to being nervous as hell over the proceedings taking so long, until my stomach was turning cartwheels every time the coded three knocks came to the door. Just as another three taps came with Ralph opening the door while still knocking.

"You're up, pal!" Ralph announced.

This time he was accompanied by two goons, one stood next to Ralph as the other walked in and patted me down from head to toe before I was allowed to leave the room. It was honestly the first time I had second thoughts as to whether Ralph was an actual butler or held some higher position of power. Maybe I was making too much of his assignment, but I could not see the mob allowing a simple butler to know as much as he did about the inner works of such an elaborate meeting.

Then again, maybe Ralph was in retirement like Andrew and just enjoyed staying close to the action. I mean these guys never really lost their status — once a Don always a Don. Their families still got a cut from the business from here to Italy. They just did not receive as much as an active boss received, but when you're in retirement, who cares because you still collect without ever having to get your hands dirty.

"You're about to make history kid," Ralph said,

patting me on my back as I stepped out of the room. "Let's hope so Ralph, let's hope so."

☙

Except for the absence of media and scrambling film-taking reporters, the room I was escorted to looked like something your see on CSPAN. I had stepped into the room where the big sharks gave the little piranhas the right to swim in the ocean.

There was a full panel of some of the most notorious mobsters from a across the globe. Age had taken its toll on most of them but not even age could demean the bite these men — and now woman — possessed. A hand was placed on my shoulder by one of the goons to halt my advance as we stepped into the room to be seated, and the gentlemen seated was about to get out of the chair. From the tension in the room and his body language, he had been scolded, or at least from the last few words I caught entering the room, it wasn't pleasant for him.

"And I caution you Mr. Sobrinos," one speaker continued, "to honor the decision handed down to you by this Commission."

"Yes Sir, Mr. Chairman," he responded, straightening his jacket as he was preparing to be dismissed.

"You're free to leave," the Chairman said.

The man shot past me and out the door with beads of sweat atop his forehead, and did not look left nor right leaving the room.

"Who's next?" the Chairman asked, looking down at a folder in front of him.

"Michigan," was announced by an unknown suit.

"Michigan?" he asked, then looked at the end of the table.

"Take the seat up front," the goon whispered into my ear.

I did as I was told. "Yes, that would be Mr. Lion of Detroit, Mr. Chairman." It was Ferrell's voice speaking into the mic.

He looked at me from the top of his glasses, then did a double take. "Oh yes," he said, "Mr. Lion."

It would be perhaps unwise to say what I saw sitting before the committee, and names were not important if you knew who ran countries like Columbia, Peru, China, Afghanistan, Czechoslovakia, just to name a few, and the likes of Russia. I took my seat wondering how Homeland Security had most if, not all, of these men flagged and yet they still managed to get into the country. These are men that were drug warlords and on the FBI or CIA's Most Wanted list. Some weren't seated at the table but sat directly behind the person seating in their chair. Let's just say, to mention some of these men's names could spell a death sentence for utter ignorance and not thinking twice before speaking.

"Mr. Lion, is it?" the Chairman asked.

"Ah," I cleared my throat. "Good afternoon. Yes sir, Mr. Chairman," I said. "That's correct."

"Who's sponsoring Mr. Lion before the Commission?"

"The Legion Family," Ferrell said, and it was the first time I noticed Andrew and David behind her.

It was a lot of shuffling of papers, covering microphones as they spoke to each other. David was helping Andrew out of his chair, and he got to the mic. Up until then, I was getting a bad reading from the room. He just touched Ferrell on the shoulder and sat back down with the help of David. That was it, that was all it took for the room to fall dead silent.

"Is there a second?" the Chairman asked.

Nothing. . ."Cisneros, will second," came from the other side of the room. He looked over at Ferrell and nodded his head. At best guess, he had just laid a marker or paying a debt owed to the Valentinos. Whichever it was, I was pretty sure I'd be seeing him again.

"Very well," the chairman said. "I would propose we adjourn the vote until after lunch if there's going to be any objections."

No one objected.

"Very well, then we will continue," he said. "Mr. Lion is before the committee today after having spent many years with the Valentino family. Do you understand the purpose of the Commission, Mr. Lion?"

"Yes I do."

"Have you ever been a part of another Commission that we should know about?"

"No, sir."

The Q & A went on for forty-five minutes.

"Do you understand that the areas you operate in cannot be expanded without the committee's approval?"

"Yes, sir Mr. Chairman."

"Have you ever worked in law enforcement?"

"Never."

And questions were asked about the Lion family of Michigan and would it be a merger with the Legion family. A vote was put to the floor, and no one used their veto power.

"Mr. Lion," the Chairman said, "let me be the first to welcome you into the family with us."

"Thank you, Mr. Chairman," I said, looking over at Ferrell wearing a joyous smile. "You're free to go," he ended.

I stood up feeling ten foot tall. I had on a ring that gave me the power most men would never come close to ever knowing. Ferrell was not only the first woman to ever be seated on the Commission, but I was the first Black man to ever become a Don in America. I had seen the world change when Barack Obama became the first Black man as President of the United States, and four years later after Donald Trump's one term as President, Kamala Harris became the first Black female vice-president in America the same year.

Leaving the room had a different feeling than when I was searched going in, and no matter what was thought of me going in, coming away from the Commission made me untouchable.

⟨✧⟩

MOTTO OF THE UNDERWORLD: Survival knows no laws. If caught committing a crime, deny everything. Even if caught red-handed standing over a corpse with the smoking gun in your hand, deny having the gun by denying your hand.

Chapter 34

CODE OF CONDUCT 101. PROTECT THE COMMISSION BY denial of its existence, even its members.

That was the very first page I thumbed to in the Code of the Commission (underground handbook) after it was handed to me, or actually, it was in my room when I came back from my induction. The difference this time was the door was left open and unguarded. Every boss of bosses was required to know every law in the book and the book was not to be removed from the estate, as what the last page read. It wasn't that large and I saw no harm in taking pics of it in my iPhone to be read when I could focus more attention to its pages.

It was just after 1:45 P.M., so I sat by the window and read some of the rules I was now sworn to honor, but mostly I just sat there waiting for Ferrell to complete her business at the table, thinking how fast the both of us rose to power, especially Ferrell. She had a seat unlike the Brotherhood, because the families that sat at the Brotherhood's table was limited as to what could be accomplished. Inside of the Commission book, it spoke a lot about the Pope. Donations were required, for what, I could not answer but I did know one thing — when Pope Francis spoke it reverberated around the world.

"Now aren't you happy I made you stay?" Ferrell said, entering the room and startling me a bit.

I stood from my chair and turned to face her.

"You looked very important sitting at the table, shot caller," I said, holding my hand up in the air.

"That's because I am," she said, holding her hand up as well.

We both fist-bumped our rings.

"You might just be."

"I got you in didn't I," and the fist bump wasn't enough, so she came in for a kiss. "I wanted to jump over the table and be the first to congratulate you but the chairman beat me to it."

"I don't think a kiss from him would have been very welcome."

She laughed, and more kisses.

"Is this what it cost me?"

"It's a start."

That was not a tall order and I was happy to be celebrating my status with someone who expressed more joy over the idea than I did.

"Only a boss of bosses can kiss like that."

"How many guys in the world can say they've kissed a First Lady-boss of bosses?"

"Come on, let's get you home to pay your respects to Pharaoh."

"What happened to Andrew?" I asked, gathering my things and following Ferrell out of the room.

"He's in a closed conference meeting."

"I wanted to thank him."

"You already have. And don't worry the Commission knows why we're leaving."

In the hallway just before we stepped outside, Ferrell turned around to face me.

"Here, try this on," she said, handing my watch back to me. I started to put it on. "No, read the inside first."

Don Lion of Michigan from Italy.

"Thank you."

"You'll get to do that later."

We were out of the door and headed to the airport with what I came for. The Lion family ring was now legendary and recognized internationally. Michigan had become known for more than the Cotton Club, the Brotherhood was right up the street.

Whoever said, what you don't know can't hurt you, lied! Because what you don't know can kill you.

Chapter 35

USE THE HAND OF A SNAKE TO CATCH A SNAKE IS THE first rule heads of state and powerful leaders learn to never get caught with soiled hands.

"I never thought I would miss this state so much," Ferrell said from the passenger's seat in my car that was left in the airport hangar on my flight to Massachusetts, as we headed back to her mansion.

"Mum."

"What are you thinking about, Don Lion?"

"Business."

"No time to celebrate, just back to business?"

"Something like that."

"Is this business about your uncle?"

"You can say that."

"So let me guess, now you're taking me home."

"Isn't that where you want to go after a long trip?"

"You're not dropping me there alone, Lion."

"Look, Ferrell..." "No, don't you even try to dismiss me from what you're going through like I'm some random stranger. Your family is my family now and if you're going to see Pharaoh, then I'm going as well."

I began swerving through traffic, "I'm not going to see Pharaoh."

"If you're not, then where are we going?"

"Why don't we go to the house get something to eat and talk about this then, okay?"

"I'm not frail Lion, I've seen deceased people before."

"I just told you I'm not going to see Pharaoh."

"Wait, you're saying you're not going at all?"

"No I'm not."

That was the only answer that brought some silence in the car, for a few minutes anyway.

"I don't understand," she said. "Don't you want to pay your respect to your uncle?"

"I'm about to pay my respect in another way."

The traffic began to clear up for most of the drive, and for a moment I wished my problems were behind me as opposed to being a storm straight ahead and I was driving right into it with Ferrell fighting me to stay by my side.

"Why does hearing you say that scare me?"

I didn't respond.

"I know I'm supposed to be tough and all by being a mob boss, but I'm still a girl with feelings."

"What do you want me to say?"

"I don't know, anything. Just don't shut down on me, because that scares me most and makes me feel like I'm alone to sort things out."

I came up off the highway feeling sort of like an inconsiderate asshole. Ferrell was trying to be there for a grieving man who had lost a family member, but instead I was fixated on vengeance, and all she wanted was for me to be patient enough to explain what it was I was planning.

"There's some people I need to see to get some answers from, and these people won't be happy to see me coming. I'm just trying to protect you."

"I hope that wasn't supposed to make me feel better because now it stresses me more to know that you want to drop me off and head into danger."

"I don't know what to tell you other than that this is very important to me. Our business is intertwined and your brother knew that and knew when to let me handle my business which you must learn the difference between the two."

As we pulled up to the mansion, Ferrell went for the glove compartment, pulled out the remote control, opened the gate and put it back in the compartment.

I didn't know what to say to that so I said nothing. It was starting to feel like we were in a relationship than it being a business partnership. I pulled up to the house and we both just sat there.

Finally Ferrell opened her door, "I'll get out, but you know what?" She gathered some of her things. "I'm not Andrew, and this is a new partnership that you better start getting used to things running a whole lot differently, and one of them is you getting used to me being attached to your trigger!" she said forcefully. "Let's not forget of all the years you've been with Andrew, it was me that brought you into — a family he never considered giving equal power alongside him."

Ferrell made a point I could not contest, so I sat and listened patiently.

"You represent," she went on to say, "everything Andrew and David wishes they could be. Your strength is feared all over the world, but until now it was not linked to the families of nations. Don't think your strength means you can do this on your own. You're the hand of a snake that they use to catch other snakes."

"There's a side of me you don't want to know."

"That's not true," she got out of the car. "What part of what I just said don't you understand?! Who you are is more of a mystery to yourself than you think you are to others, Lion." She slammed the door shut and stormed up the steps.

I backed out of the driveway before the gate could completely shut and it almost scraped my front end, which was a reckless move to try to beat the gate closing. Sometimes the worst time to get hit with the truth is when you're running from yourself.

⁂

Everything about how I moved was complicated and would require too much energy to explain to Ferrell why I moved the way I did. She was extremely inquisitive about everything. Not that it was a bad thing, but some situations you can't rush into with someone you care about because it becomes a distraction to watch out for them instead of paying attention to what needed to be focused on.

"Hello," Je'Niece answered the phone.

"Are you smiling?" I asked.

"How did you know?" she asked. "I mean it's crazy because I was just thinking about you, hoping you'd call."

"Is that a fact?"

"Where are you?"

"Heading to your house if you're home."

"You're just saying that."

"Is your car working?"

"Nah, kinda, sorta," she laughed. "Why?"

"Because I want to borrow it."

"Use it, something wrong with your car?"

"No, it works just fine."

"Then why —" She stopped herself. "Forget I asked. Is that the only reason you called me?"

"Actually I just got back in town."

"Don't tell me you're being a super spreader."

"No, I practice safe traveling."

"How is that possible?"

"Private jet."

"Excuse me, now I'm really mad at you for not taking me."

I laughed. "Did you take Medina and that's why you didn't take me on your private jet?"

I had other reasons for calling Je'Niece and almost forgot about her direct approach. All of my problems faded as I sped up the highway talking to her.

"We weren't supposed to hook up until New Year's Eve, remember?"

"No!" she shot back. "I remember saying not to keep me waiting for a call from you."

Mentioning Medina's name brought her to mind and caused me to pause in thought. She threw me out of my house, and I didn't know how much time I should wait before going back.

"Y'all had a fight didn't y'all?" JeNiece asked.

"What makes you say that?" I asked, surprised.

"Because you got too quiet when I said her name."

"Nah, we good."

"Don't be lying to me," she said flatly. "If you don't want to talk about it, just say that and I can respect that but we gonna keep it one hundred unless you scared of me."

I almost didn't know where to go with that.

"Yeah, she's upset with me. Is that better?"

"Did you tell her about me?"

Should I have?"

"You told me about her so why not?"

"Actually you asked about her and if she asked about you, I'd be just as truthful."

Je'Niece popped her lips. "Okay if you say so."

I laughed. "You're a cold piece, you know that?"

"You coming to warm me up?" she said in a sexy tone.

"It'll have to wait."

"You better 'cause once it gets hot, you gonna have your hands full."

Je'Niece was starting to move things beyond my reasons for

coming to see her, and if I did not slow things down she would have me totally distracted by the time I got there.

"Look here," I said. "I'll be at your doorstep in a few minutes and I won't be coming inside, so listen for my horn and bring me your keys, alright?"

"Okay mystery man," she said. "I'll be sitting in the window waiting for you."

"See you in a few minutes."

"What are you about to do that you can't talk to me until you get here?"

"I am here, turning the corner right now."

"Oh then bye."

"Bye." I hung up.

Seconds later, just like she said, the curtain fell closed as I pulled up in front of the house. The front door swung open and Je'Niece popped out wearing a blue jean mini shirt that buttoned down in the front, a diamond studded Divine Diva hoodie, and Uggs on her feet. She tiptoed down the steps with her arms folded suggesting she was cold and jumped inside the car with a set of keys balled up in her hands.

"Whooo," she shivered. "It's too cold to be out here." She handed me her car keys.

"Which one is yours?" I asked.

"Take a guess."

"It better not be that piece of junk Mustang."

"Oh no, you didn't!" she said, pushing me in a joking manner. "That's still my babe even though it's a hoody."

I looked at the car having serious doubts about getting under the wheel and trusting its reliability.

"Well, I just hope your baby don't stop on me in the middle of the road."

"It ain't that messed up."

"Then what's wrong with it?"

"Do I look like a mechanical engineer?"

I looked down at her waxed legs and long finger nails, turned the engine off and handed her the keys.

"Don't play, are you seriously giving me your keys?"

"Yes, I'm serious but there's one catch."

"What," she said, taking the keys slowly in her hand.

"I don't want you to be joy-riding around in this neighborhood."

"Then where else Imma go?"

"You don't have friends and family elsewhere?"

"Yeah."

"Then go visit them."

"Ain't nobody gonna shoot me up, are they?"

"No, it's not like that."

"Then what is it, you don't want anyone to know I'm your girlfriend?"

"Who said anything about you being my woman?"

"Nobody but that's what they will say by seeing me driving your car around."

"I don't give a fuck about what anybody has to say about seeing you in this car. I'm just asking you to keep a low profile until I am done taking care of the business I'm on. No one knows your car and I don't want them to see me coming."

"I see why everyone is so afraid of you."

"Why's that?"

"You came all the way over here in a good car to get in my piece of junk," Je'Niece said. "Most guys would laugh at the idea of changing keys."

"So we agree you won't be flossing in the hood, right?"

"Yes, I heard you," she said. "I like this mask, you got any more like this?"

"In the glove compartment, now I just have one question."

"What's that?"

"You said you see why people are afraid of me. Are you afraid of me?"

"No, I'm not afraid of you but I am afraid of what it is you do."

We both got out of the car. "I'll call you later," I said as I walked across the street to Je'Niece's Mustang and she got to the top of her steps and stood there with her arms folded watching me.

I got inside and it took four tries before the engine started, puttered and cut off on me. The fifth time it started, and I had to give it some gas to keep it running. I honked the horn, feeling proud that I managed to get the car out of park and rolling down the road as I switched gears. Je'Niece laughed and waved goodbye and rushed inside the house.

⁂

Later that evening...

I sat out in front of Holiday's house and dozed off, for how long I did not know but his tapping on the passenger's window woke me up. I unlocked the door and he got inside.

"God damn Lion, you trying to get killed sitting out here like this?"

I did not notice the gun in his hand until he laid it in his lap.

"I did not know if you were in or not with all the lights out so early."

"Did knocking on the door cross your mind?"

"I was going to knock but I must have dozed off."

"So why are you out here sleeping in front of my house in this piece of junk?"

"You decided not to take that vacation?"

"A vacation is when you get away from the people you work with every day, and wherever the Crazy-Eight go trouble follows us," he said. "But I know you didn't drive over here to talk about my vacation time so what's the mission, big man?"

I went in my pocket and pulled out a plane ticket I picked up before leaving Massachusetts, and an envelope with fifty grand inside.

"Florida?" he said, looking at the ticket.

"Florida," I repeated.

"Who the fuck you got beef with all the way down in Florida?"

"Address is written on the back of the ticket," I said. "This is solo-dolo. You make it back, there's a bonus in it for you."

Holiday looked at me then inside the envelope. "Are you serious?"

"You up for it or should I keep it moving?"

He shook his head from side to side. "These Italians you going after. You know what this means if it comes back on our doorstep, right?"

"I know what it means, you just make sure what happens down south stays down south."

"That gun's got any sentimental value to you?"

"If it did I wouldn't be out here with it ready to use it, it's a burner."

I leaned over and opened the glove compartment. "Leave it on your way out."

Holiday, placed the 9mm in the glove compartment, closed it and opened the passenger's door and got out. "That bonus better include someplace I can get out of dodge for at least a couple years."

"I'll throw in an island that stays hot all year round."

Holiday closed the door and didn't look back.

<hr/>

My stick shift driving was a little rusty starting out, but after driving from one side of town to the other, I was popping the clutch and shifting gears like the Mustang was mine. I pulled into my Grosse Pointe driveway and went in from the back door.

Something was out of place; a glass of cognac was sitting on the dining room table. I thought maybe I left it there but then the toilet flushed. I instantly thought about the 9mm in the glove compartment and going back out to the car and retrieve it, but I scanned around the room and saw nothing was out of place. Instead, I picked up a candle holder from the center of the table and began making my way towards the back of the house. I arched it above my head just as I was about to turn into the hallway, took a deep breath and…"Oh shit!" Ferrell jumped back and grabbed her chest.

"Ferrell, what the hell are you doing here?!" I yelled but lowering the candle holder.

For someone who was in someone else's house, she looked shocked to see me, and then started laughing.

"You almost just got your head bashed in and you think it's funny?"

"I'm sorry," she said between laughing and still holding her chest. "I did not mean to scare you."

"Scare me," I shook the candle in the air. "Do I look scared?"

"You had to see your face," she went on to say with tears in her eyes and wiping them away.

"What are you doing here anyway, and how did you get in here?"

Ferrell finally composed herself long enough to say, "I used the back slide door that you never lock. Remember before we left, I asked if you were you going to lock it, so I knew it would be open," she answered and started walking towards the dining room for her drink. I followed behind her and had to grab her by the arm.

"Wait."

"What is it?" she asked.

"Do you think it's okay to invite yourself into my home without my permission?"

"You're hurting me, Lion. Now will you let go of my arm?"

"After you answer my question I will."

Ferrell sat her drink down and dug her nails into my forearm until I let her go. "Why are you being so mean to me? I did not kill Pharaoh and I could not stay in that house after the way you talked to me and just left me alone. I just wanted to surprise you and to say I'm sorry for not being more considerate for what you're going through."

It was too late for Ferrell to apologize and I started to tell her soon she'd come to know my pain for herself, but that would have been a death sentence by my own admittance, so I walked past her into the living room and sat down in my recliner wondering if Holiday had boarded his plane for Florida. Ferrell had David in her ear. Andrew I could handle because he was rooting for both of our success, but David was a thorn in my side. Eventually, Andrew would be gone and either he or Ferrell would try to bring David under Ferrell. I could not afford to wait and see where his envy would end.

I sat down and Ferrell took a seat on the sofa closest to me. "Have you taken care of your business?" she asked.

"Partly, I just came here to pick something up."

"So you're leaving me here alone as well?"

"I didn't bring you here so how am I leaving you here alone?" I stood up when a text message came in from Castro saying to meet him at the basement.

She got up and walked over to where she sat her drink down,

picked up the glass and before she sat back in her seat she asked, "Do you want me to fix you a drink?" then took a sip from her glass.

"Maybe later," I said, walking out of the room.

I picked up a few things and managed to go out the back without seeing Ferrell before I left back out, but I heard the bedroom door slam shut so I can only assume she intended not to get in my way.

The Mustang ran a lot better once it was warmed up and my best guess was it needed a tune-up.

⌘

I walked in on Castro talking to one of Pharaoh's surviving junkie friends and making small talk about Tom Brady and the Superbowl that was about to kick off in four hours.

"Sup, Lion?" Castro spoke.

"Who are you?" I asked the third guy in the room I didn't know.

"This is Nick Gibson," the nurse known as Doc answered for him. "He was at Henry Ford Hospital with us."

"So tell me Nick," I began, unbuttoning my full length leather coat, pulled out the 9mm I got from Holiday and sat down across from the three junkies so I could look them dead in the eyes. "What the hell happened at that hospital?"

"Look man," Nick held his fat hands in the air, "I don't know —"Those were Nick Gibson the junkie's last words, as he jerked back hard on the sofa from the impact of three bullets.

"Sit your ass down," I said to Shorty, who bounced out of

his seat as the shots rang out, piss running down his pants as he trembled so violently from fear. Doc had to pull him down in the seat, who himself was frozen with fright.

"Goddamn, Lion!" Castro said. "Not up here man."

"I told you he was gonna kill us, Jesus help us," Shorty cried out.

"Now if you don't know shit like Nick, we can save a lot of time," I laid the pistol on my thigh.Doc was the first one to speak up, "Lion, I'll tell you anything you want to know." Nick had slumped over on his shoulder, his eyes open and bloodshot red.

"Good," I said, and thought about what Castro said. "Since Nick doesn't know anything, why don't we take him to basement so he doesn't soil the sofa."

"Come on Shorty, pull it together and help me," Doc said but was almost carrying the corpse alone. Shorty's willpower may have been there, but his nerves were getting the best of him.

I led the way down to the basement with Castro following behind them. If Shorty's nerves were shot after seeing his friend killed, it was nothing compared to his reaction once he saw the lethal injection table he saw upon entering the interrogation room and dropped Nick's dead weight on Doc.

"You can drop him anywhere," I said, taking up one of the folding chairs and sitting down as Castro did the same, but closer to the entrance.

"Have a seat fellas," I said, watching them handle Nick's dead body like he was asleep and they didn't want to wake him.

"Why was drugs shot up in Pharaoh's I.V. bag?" was my first question.

"He was in pain and asked us to do it because they would not give him anything at the hospital," Doc spoke up and his sidekick nodded his head up and down in agreement, "but we wouldn't do it."

"Someone did, and I want to know who was it."

"Lion," Doc twisted in his chair as if it was going to help him get his story straight, "you know I wouldn't do anything to hurt Pharaoh."

"I had used all I had so I couldn't give him nothing," Shorty found the nerve to speak.

"For what it's worth," I said, "I know both of you were close friends to Pharaoh."

"We got him to the hospital."

"And abandoned him."

"I'm sorry Lion, but I didn't know what else to do.."

My own words flashed back to me when just days before I walked in on Shorty about to overdose and I suggested they throw him in a vacant house if he died. It angered me that he was sitting in front of me alive and Pharaoh, who they fed off of, was dead. I wanted to kill them both because someone needed to be held accountable.

"So what do you think?" I turned the interrogation over to Castro.

"It's your call," he said. "They can't tell us what they don't know."

"Neither could Nick," I said.

Everyone looked at the slumped over body.

"So this is what you're going to do," I said. "If this comes back on the two of you, then you'll end up joining Pharaoh and Nick right here. Until I find out who shot that dope into his bag, I won't rest."

Castro gestured me off to the side.

"What's up?"

"They just became loose ends, you know that right?"

I looked over my shoulder at them.

"Drill down on them and scrub it clean," I said, handing him two packets of raw and two needles, then I left the way I had arrived.

I didn't have the answers I was looking for and for that reason, no one got a free pass. The packs of dope were pure grade, a much better departure than they gave Pharaoh.

Chapter 36

AFTER LEAVING THE INTERROGATION ROOM, I GOT IN the Mustang and decided to go check on Medina and relieve Jesse so that he could look in on his family and take a hot shower in his own home, and most importantly, to check in with his wife.

Jesse met me at the front door and I knew by not knowing the Mustang he would be on guard by me pulling into the driveway.

"Hey Jesse, everything alright?"

"Now it is," he said, looking over my shoulder at the Mustang. I looked down at the tech in his hand and knew what he meant.

"Came to relieve you," I said walking into the living room as he closed and locked the door.

"Has she come down?" I asked, sitting down in the lazy boy.

"Just to fix herself some tea mostly and barely ate anything," Jesse was putting on his coat while talking.

"Alright my man," I got up to walk him to the door. "Thanks for everything," handing him an envelope.

"You're welcome," he said. "Call me when you need me on

deck."" I will," I said, holding the door open as Jesse got in his car and left. I then closed the door and locked it.

I was slightly startled when I turned around after locking the door and saw Medina standing behind me.

"Hi," she said, standing there with my robe on and locked it tight from my ability to see her goodies.

"Hey," I responded.

"What are you doing here?"

"Covering for Jesse until he gets back."

"Oh," she said, looking around. "He's gone?"

"Yeah, he just left, unless you want me to leave or I could stay outside."

"I'm supposed to be mad at you," Medina replied.

She started to say something, but nothing came out.

"You can stay inside, I guess," she looked at me, "but I thought I told you not to come back here."

"I tried to stay away but it wasn't working out too good."

"I know," she said, "I was thinking about how bad you are for me and I even tried to find a reason why I should never see you again." She paused. "But all I could think about was what would my life be like without you in it. I don't know, I can't stand being with you with your lifestyle and I can't seem to break my thoughts away from you even though I want to. Does that make sense?" she asked, and walked over to the sofa and sat down, and I sat beside her.

"You want me to answer that?"

"Yes, but I don't want you to do that thing you always do."

"What thing?"

"I try to tell you something and somehow you take over the conversation and change my mind."

"I understand what you mean."

"Good, so just let me say what I want to say from my own head okay, and then you can respond."

I nodded in agreement.

Medina took a deep breath. "I know that I can't change you Lion, and I don't know if I would if I could, but I know that I can't live with you the way you live your life. It's dangerous and I can't handle it. I mean, sometimes you make me wish that I was more, you know, like one of those ride-or-die chicks. I even envy them because I know that they can identify with what it is you're going through more than I can. I'm sorry that you've had it so hard in life and I know that everything that you do is a result of how much you've struggled and your anger is because you feel you've been forced to make the decisions you've made."

I sat there listening to Medina and everything she needed to get off her chest and some of which were expressed better than I could describe of my own life. What she was able to articulate with words, I only knew how to put into actions. If only words could pay my bills, support the countless families that relied on me to put food on their tables like Jesse, and only if Medina's words could change the things I'd already done, I would have wholly embraced the person she wanted to love, marry and spend her life with.

"You're a very dangerous man Lion, and my fear is I don't know if you're capable of not being the person you've allowed yourself to become," she added. "I know that you're not good for me and I somehow allowed you to convince me that everything I know about you isn't what I know to be true. You make me feel everything I've never felt for a man. I want to see you when I can't stand the sight of you, love you when I should hate you, and I even cry myself to sleep most nights because I can't feel you inside of me and I know you're somewhere else doing things that could end your life and that's too heavy of a burden to carry on my soul. Don't you feel me calling out to you when you're out in those streets, Lion?" she asked, wiping tears from her

eyes. "You have to help me, Lion. Help me get over you or help me to help you change who you are right now. I've tried to be patient and to wait for you to find another way to live but you seem to keep finding ways to dig yourself in deeper and deeper and I'm afraid at some point, you're going to dig yourself in so deep until there will be no way out for you."

I balled my fist that held the Legion family ring on my finger. It was too late; I was already in so deep there was no way out for me. Even as Medina and I sat there pondering the future, Holiday was heading to Florida, after ordering a hit on another family member. That alone drew me in to the point of no return.

"Now you can respond," she said.

You know I love you," I started.

"No no-no," Medina shook her head from side to side, tears falling heavy. "Wait please," she begged. "Why have you waited until now to tell me you love me when I've waited so long to hear you say it?" The question was met by more tears.

"Medina, if it was not for my lifestyle, the chances of us

meeting would have been slim at best, and I wouldn't belong here to have gotten close to you if it wasn't for who I've become."

"All you have to do is walk away, change, and we can start over."

"I can't start over Medina."

"Yes you can... We can."

"No," I shook my head, looking down at the ring. "We can't." I looked at her. "They will never let me out."

"Who won't let you out?"

"It doesn't matter."

"Yes it does... If you want me to understand."

"Because I can't get out even if I wanted to."

"So you're saying you don't want to, is that what you're saying?" She wiped her eyes, and her question became aggressive.

"They'll kill me if I try to leave," I reluctantly said.

Medina's face softened and a mixture of compassion as well as fear was in her eyes.

"We can go to the police," she proposed. "They'll put us in a witness protective program," she said as if it was a genius idea.

"Baby, that can only happen if I testify against someone."

"You can do that."

"No."

"You can't or you won't do it?"

"That would require me to testify against myself and I won't implicate myself committing any crimes."

"Then we can leave the country, Lion."

"It's over Medina."

"What?... What are you saying?"

231

"I'm saying neither one of us can go on like this. I can't change what has already been set in motion."

Medina dropped her head and started to mumble something to herself, then said, "I have something I want to show you if that's not asking too much."

"No, it's not asking too much. What is it?"

"It's upstairs," she stood up. "Give me a few minutes before you come up."

"Alright," I said and sat there for a few minutes thinking of what it could be she wanted to show me. I didn't want to walk away from our relationship and thought about how I could turn things around to convince her that what we had was worth holding onto. Maybe we both needed to sleep on it, at least that's what I was thinking as I got up and headed upstairs to what it was she wanted to show me.

"Medina!" I called out to let her know I was coming up, and it was then I heard a single gunshot ring out from upstairs.

"Medina!" I yelled and started leaping the stairs two at a time until I reached to top landing, slid across the wooden floor and had to regain my balance. "Medina!" I yelled, but it was too late. I could see her laying on the bathroom floor as I cleared the bedroom door and ran into the bathroom. The gun was mine, kept in the safe box in my closet.

"Lion," she said, as I got down on the floor and took her in my arms.

"What did you do?" I took the gun from her hand and dropped it on the floor, then tried to brush the blood from her face. "I'm here, right here I got you," I said. "I'll change, we can leave the country I promise, just don't leave me! Medina! Medina, say something."

"I lov-lov-love you, Lion," she said, trying to reach up to touch my face.

"I know, I love you too babe," I grabbed her hand and put it on my face. "I'm sorry. I'm so sorry."

"I killed a man," she said, choking on her own blood.

"No-no, he was a bad man, you had no choice. It wasn't your fault," I kept wiping the blood away from her face and I couldn't see where she shot herself, it wouldn't stop.

"No, I have..." she was coughing up blood. "...to say this." Medina struggled. "It's too hard to live with what I did and I-i-i..." "Jesse!!! Jesse!!!"" I looked for my phone. "Wait, hold on baby. I'll get some help, just stay with me Medina." But she started jerking violently and gargling in her blood until her body went limp in my arms.

I dropped my phone to the floor, grabbed the drying towel from the towel rack and cleaned the blood off her beautiful face. "Medina," I whispered in her ear as my tears of love mixed with her blood of sorrow, but she was gone.

We sat there for a long time, occasionally her leg or arm would jerk. I didn't know what to do but hold her in my arms and to keep wiping the blood from her face.

Okay, I got to pull it together, I told myself. I couldn't call the police to my house. I picked Medina up and carried her to the bed and went back to get the gun and my phone from the bathroom. I put the pistol next to Medina and wrapped her in the blanket.

I had to pull the car inside of the garage, so that's what I did.

I had to get her body out of there before sunrise. I could not see putting Medina in the trunk nor was it wise to have a dead body sitting in the passenger's seat. "The backseat will be safe," I said out loud. Once I got her to the garage, the blanket was soaked through and so I laid her on the hood of the car, got a leaf bag and put her inside of it, then used some duct tape to keep her fluids from leaking all over the place. The Mustang was a small two-seater, and it was hell trying to get Medina in the backseat, so I got her in on one side and had to go around to the other side to pull her fully in. I had to go back inside after looking at myself and change clothes. I was just as soaked in Medina's blood as the blanket had become. I put the bloody clothes in a bag and tossed them in the backseat, then backed out of the garage with the Mustang carrying dead weight.

⟬⟭

At the halfway point in reaching West Bloomfield, it felt like I had committed murder and had the pistol and body of evidence in the car with me.

I had made it to Medina's house without detection and no one was moving on her block. I pulled in the driveway and got as close to the door as I possibly could without looking suspicious, got out, and got the keys from the mailbox where Major said they'd be.

⟬⟭

If police came knocking, it was the only way to know if I managed to get Medina inside the house undetected.

I put her on the bed, ripped the plastic from her body and unwrapped the blanket. I couldn't leave her looking the way she did, mouth gaped open, hair matted with blood and the soiled robe. I collapsed on the side of the bed next to her and decided there was only one thing left to do.

I got up and went into Medina's closet, pulled out her favorite gown, and laid it out on the chair. Went to the kitchen and got a bucket, and filled it with warm water in the bathroom, got a sponge and took the robe off her and gave her a sponge bath. I left her underclothing on to make it look like your typical suicide. As if she had planned the whole thing and laid down on the bed to be released from this world. I put the blanket, robe, sponge, and bucket inside the leaf bag, then laid the pistol inside her hand after wiping it clean. I thought about writing a suicide note but on second thought, I didn't want my own penmanship left behind.

I gave the only woman I ever told I love her, perhaps too late a kiss and left the house for the last time remembering the first time Medina had invited me over for dinner, drinks and a dish movie. I locked the door and left the best part of me behind to be discovered by the coroner

Chapter
37

WOODWARD AVENUE IN DETROIT WAS BEST KNOWN for its Motor City classic car show and fine whores. The whores that strolled the avenue were just as fine as the old model cars, those that kept themselves up anyway, and were twice as deadly if you got hit by one.

I pulled into a 24/7 self-carwash the whores had make into their quickie spot and must have thought I was a mark looking for a quick trick. I had the doors open, seats flipped forward and was cleaning anything that could tie the Mustang back to Medina.

"You looking for some help?" A voice came from the other side of the open door.

"Naw, I'm good," I said without looking up and was pulling all sorts of trash from beneath the seat.

"Damn, somebody vomit in here," she said, leaning in the backseat, "or shitted on them self."

I stopped and looked up at the nosey whore. The only thing

I found of interest was the whore's nose, and I was glad it was her nose and not Je'Niece who asked what happened inside the car.

"You must be new around here," she said as I stood up and looked at her over the roof of the car.

"Not at all," I said.

"Then we gonna just stand here looking at each other or get out of the cold?"

"What's your name?" I asked as I flipped the car seat back.

"Monica, but everyone calls me Moe."

"Okay Moe, I'm Lion."

Monica took a step away from my car and almost twisted her ankle in doing so. "The Westside Lion?" she asked.

"Well, we are on the westside, and I am the Lion," I smiled.

A look is worth a thousand words.

Monica did a double take looking in the backseat. "I'm sorry Mr. Lion, I didn't recognize you or I would have minded my own business. Really, I apologize, okay?" She turned and walked off as fast as her legs could move.

The quarters I had put in the vacuum ran out, so I hung the hose on the hook and got into the car not knowing how to take what had just happened. I pulled up to the curve, hit my turn signal and saw Monica look back and stumble again in her high heels. I pulled out into traffic and hit the horn as I sped past Monica. I looked in the rearview to see her waving, then leaned on the wall of the liquor store she was about to pass.

Brent was under the hood of a piped-out 1970 candy-painted Monte Carlo when I pulled up to the junkyard. He looked over at me, did a double take, went back to whatever he was doing under the hood and shook his head from side to side.

Several minutes later, he came over to the Mustang, wiping his hands on a grease rag he had taken from his back pocket, opened the passengers door with the same rag and got inside, and closed the door with the same rag.

"Damn, Big Dawg," he said. "Somebody —""Don't even say it," I cut him off.

"Well shit," he said, going in his pocket. "I know you don't like me smoking in your ride but I got to light something up in here or roll down the window."

"Go right ahead."

"You been very busy lately, huh?" he said, taking a long drag from the wood, then held it out offering me a hit.

"Do you need more money for this job?" I said, ignoring his rambling.

"It ain't about the money, you always taken good care of me."

"Okay, then I don't want to talk about something that's a done deal. Tell me what's it going to cost me to get out of this car, walk across that street, get me a paper, something to eat, and how long is it going to take for you to pop the tags out of this car and into another?"

"You're in luck today, Big Dawg," he said, looking at the envelope on the console.

I opened the car door and got out while he was still talking.

"Couple hours!" he yelled, which meant thirty minutes. He'll stand around smoking or working on another car for the other hour and a half.

"One hour, Brent!" I put up one finger.

Popping a vent number out of the dashboard and the side door is all it took to put Je'Niece in a new-used vehicle. It was an older model car so the authorities wouldn't suspect it to be a tag job.

Chapter 38

CONEY ISLAND HAS ALWAYS BEEN A FAST-FOOD CHOICE
of mine when eating on the move.

I walked several blocks up the road from the junkyard to
the Coney Island, slid in a booth, picked up the newspaper that
someone left behind, and waited to be served. A radio played
from overhead speakers, "Love is a Battlefield" was playing by
Pat Benatar when the waitress came to my booth.

"Hi, I'm Angie and I'll be taking your order," the waitress
named Angie said as she approached the table. "Ready to order?"

"Sure," I said, without taking my eyes off the article talking
about the former mayor of Detroit receiving a commutation
from President Donald Trump. "What do you recommend?" I
folded the paper and looked up at her.

"The bacon omelette and crispy hash browns."

"Add a black coffee and it's a deal."

She scribbled the order down with the pencil she pulled from
her hair. "I'll be right back with your order."

"Thank you," I said and returned to my paper.

"Here you go," Angie said, pouring a cup of coffee in a cup. "Your order will be ready in a few minutes," she smiled. "You're a new face around here."

"Yes I am," I responded, looking at the clock over Angie's shoulder to match the time with my watch.

"Oh, what a lovely watch," observant Angie said, leaning closer to look at its face.

"Thank you."

"My father used to say you can always tell how serious a man is by the time he keeps."

"Sounds like a wise man."

"He was," Angie said, and a small bell rung. "That's your order, I'll be back in a jiffy."

Moments later, Angie came back with my breakfast and more small conversation. I took a fork full of the omelette and agreed with Angie that it was a good choice, then she rushed off to serve other customers, occasionally glancing in my direction. I held my hand up and caught her attention and she rushed right over.

"Will that be it?" she asked.

"Actually I was wondering if you have an extra pencil, I've always said if I could find the time, I'd try doing a Sudoku."

"Oh wow," Angie said, patting the pocket on her apron and came out with a pencil. "Those are addictive." She held out the pencil."

Thank you, I'll be sure to give it back."

"You're very welcome. I hope you enjoy it." The bell rung for another order and Angie excused herself again, then returned moments later and refilled my cup of coffee with a smile and left.

I sat there watching the clock, sipping my coffee, and trying to figure out the number system of Sudoku.

"Are you waiting for someone?" Angie asked after watching me for an hour.

I went in my pocket and put a hundred dollar bill on the table, and pushed it across the table.

"I didn't mean that," she apologized.

"More like something," I said.

She looked confused. "My car is just up the street being repaired."

Really," she seemed relieved by my reason. "And here I thought you were about to stick the place up."

We both laughed.

"I was wondering how many cases of those hash browns could I get away with."

That tickled Angie's fancy.

"But I must get out of your hair, Angie."

"Just when I was beginning to enjoy your company," she said.

I slid out of the booth and stood in front of Angie, and returned her borrowed pencil.

She blushed and said, "If you want to finish your puzzle you can keep it. I mean I have another one."

"No, why don't you take it and maybe I'll come back to borrow it again."

Angie took the pencil from my hand, "I'll keep it sharpened for you then."

"Do that," I said, and walked out of the restaurant leaving Angie standing at the booth until I got to the door and looked back to see she had not moved until we made eye contact.

"Wait!" she said, rushing towards me. "Your change."

"Keep it as a tip."

"I'd rather know your name," Angie said, with the hundred dollar bill in her hand.

I went in my pocket and pulled out a twenty dollar bill. "Can I use your pencil?"

She pulled it from her apron. I took the hundred dollars and wrote my name, Lion (313) 451-1969, and gave her both the bills and her pencil.

Chapter 39

OUTSIDE THE AMERICAN AUTO PART'S BRENT AND HIS crew stood around Je'Niece's tagged 5.0 Mustang with rags polishing off the aged dust that had settled on it from being in the junkyard. It was a little sunburnt but had no dents or rust to the body.

Aside from the paint fading, I could have walked up to the car in any parking lot and thought it was Je'Niece original car.

"Big Dawg!" Brent said, looking proud of himself with eyes redder than a jalapeño red pepper.

"Hey dude," another one of his auto partners looking up from wiping the car down spoke.

I did not respond back, just looked at the rag he was using which was filled with smut and oil.

"You owe me big time for this one, Big Dawg," Brent said. "Now ain't no way you could have found a Mustang damn near the same color as your old car," he pointed out. "We just took the front end off your car and put it on this one and the trunk that was rusted on this one, but aside from that, yeah. And the sounds were missing so your old shit was put in here. You got yourself a nice running hoop-d."

"You plan on running yourself a used car lot?" I said, taking the keys and paperwork from his hand.

Only a grease monkey could find such joy in a thing they found joy in accomplishing. Or maybe it was so much marijuana smoke to the lungs.

"Your numbers went in smooth, and I had to file down the one on the frame and engine, but you to go."

I inspected the car by popping the hood, which was surprisingly clean. People trashed cars for all sorts of reasons or just want to get rid of an old car. I slammed the hood down.

"Everything fit like glove," Brent said. "This bitch would have sent OJ to prison it fit so good."

Maybe that was supposed to have been a joke and I was the only one who did not get it because Brent and his buddies got plenty of laughter out of it. Nevertheless, it was a good match, better seats, firmer stick shift, and the smell was gone.

"Looks good," I said to complement their work while closing the door. "Only one problem."

"What's that?" Brent asked.

The four of them stood together looking puzzled.

"The wild thang plate on the front has to go."

"No problem, Big Dawg," Brent said, and just so happened to have a screwdriver in his back pocket. "This won't take but a minute."

He ran to the front of the car and ducked out of sight for a couple of minutes and popped up with the screwdriver in one hand and the vanity plate in his other hand and rejoined his partners.

I lowered the window, "Alright fellas stay mellow."

"Come back when you want some banging sounds," one of his crew said with a mouth full of ragged teeth.

"May just take you up on that my man," I said, popped the clutch and pulled away.

I rode the streets testing everything possible in the car, lights, heater, air conditioning, brakes, speed, etc. I did not want to give the car to Je'Niece not knowing why it had been sitting in the junkyard. I turned on WJLB and the radio started playing Medina's favorite song "Butterflies" by Queen Naija. I was stuck and didn't know how to feel. She had committed suicide, and that made me angry, sad, and felt like it was my fault.

I felt numb and confused, heartbroken and lost as if I had no place to go. Every emotion inside of me wanted to get itself expressed. I wanted to go back and do things differently, pay closer attention, be a better listener, and find more time to do the things we never got to do together. I did not understand the purpose in life for working hard, making sacrifices to build a life with those we care about only to lose them and the reason for wanting to face another day, and found myself spending more time talking to the dead more than desiring conversation with the living. Maybe I should not have put Medina in the backseat of the car because now it felt like she was always behind me, and I wanted her next to me.

Another R.I.P....

Chapter 40

CHOKE OUT THE COMPETITION AND RISE TO THE TOP.

The writing was on Ferrell's face when I walked into the house and saw the look of distress on her face. Holiday had made it to Florida.

"Where were you?" Ferrell asked in a slurry speech. I looked over at the bar and saw she had turned up half a fifth of Hennessey.

"I had car trouble," I responded. "Have you moved from this spot since I left last night?"

"Andrew's dead," she said in a matter-of-fact tone, while twirling the brown liquor in her glass. She took a large gulp and started twirling its remains.

I walked over and took the glass from her hand and placed it on the coffee table, then sat down next to her.

"Did you hear what I said? Andrew's dead."

"Who told you Andrew is dead?" Something had to have gone wrong.

She picked the remote control up. "It's all over CNN."

"You heard this first by the news?"

"No, David told me."

"So David's okay?"

"He's hiding," she said. "He said he'll call when he thinks it's safe to come out of hiding."

"I was afraid something like this would happen," I said. "I'm sorry."

Ferrell looked at me puzzled. "What do you mean you were afraid this would happen?"

"I'm sorry, I shouldn't have said that." I looked Ferrell in her eyes. "It is bad timing on my part."

"No, tell me." She seemed to sober up. "I have been trying to figure this out but my brain doesn't know where to start."

"It's my fault... I did it," I confessed the truth. "I shouldn't have allowed Andrew to take me before the Commission." In order to cover up the truth, it must be woven in a lie.

"You think the Commission ordered this?"

"Let's not jump to any conclusions, but didn't you see the looks on some of the families' faces when Andrew said he would sponsor me?" I took a deep breath. "This is all my fault."

"No, don't say that Lion. If that's the case then I'm just as responsible for bringing you to the Commission."

"Damn," I whispered beneath my breath.

"I know, I feel the same way." Ferrell slid next to me and laid her head on my shoulder. "I've been crying ever since I got the call and just started drinking and waiting for you to get here. I know how you feel now about losing Pharaoh... I'm so sorry," she said, as she fell into my arms for comfort.

I lifted up and grabbed the remote and turned the news coverage off the yacht that had blown up near a dockyard.

"We have to go down there."

"And do what?" I asked.

"I don't know, something."

"There's no remains Ferrell, there's nothing to recover."

"Don't you start, Lion! Don't you fuckin' start!"

"Okay," I said, grabbing Ferrell by her shoulders. "Just listen to me for a second." I let go of her shoulders and took both her hands in my hands. "You are the boss of bosses of the Legion Family, the only remaining Valentino and it was you who second Andrew's vote to sponsor me. All I'm saying is if they got Andrew, who's to say we aren't next?"

"Why didn't they just kill you if they opposed you coming in?" she reasoned.

"Who's to say they aren't planning that very thing as we speak? I could be on that hit list and now with Andrew gone, I can't take the risk of allowing you out in the open until we find out where this came from or if it was just a gas leak."

"So what do you suggest we do?"

"For now we are going to stay in our own territory of Ohio, Chicago, and Michigan where we control the playing field until we can get to the bottom of this."

"You won't let them hurt me, right? I mean, what if they've been to the house already for me?"

249

"Don't worry about that. No one knows about this house so you're perfectly safe here."

"Is it always this crazy?"

"Normally it only happens when seats are rearranged."

Just then my iPhone went off.

"I have to take this," I said. "Hello."

"Mr. Lion."

"Yes, who is this?"

"Don Mondavi."

"Who?" I switched ears.

"Don Mondavi, Mr. Lion. We met not long ago, and I chaired over your hearing."

"Okay Don Mondavi, how can I help you?"

"We need to meet to discuss the Florida matter."

"Yeah, I heard about that. So, when and where would you like to meet?" I asked the Chairman, looking at Ferrell.

The call from Don Mondavi put me on high alert. First, I hadn't heard from Holiday, and if they had him coming out of Detroit, I would be held accountable for not knowing.

"Well," Don Mondavi said, "I would like to personally settle this as soon as possible because I have to be out of the country in the next few days, so when would be a good time for you?"

"Let me free up my schedule and get back to you with the details," I said to buy some time.

"Very well then," he said. "There isn't much we can do about this right now anyway so why don't I give you a call when I'm back from Sicily."

"That'll be great, Don."

Ferrell's eye's stretched wide as silver dollars when I said it was the Chairman.

"Is the First Lady okay?" he asked before hanging up.

"Sedated."

"I'm not good at this kind of thing. Give her my condolences please, from Don Mondavi."

"I'll do that."

"Goodbye, Don Lion."

"Good evening, Don Mondavi."

I hung up the phone not knowing what to think of the call.

"What did he want?"

"To meet."

"What? After what you've just told me, you're not going to meet with him, are you?"

"Let's just play this by ear. Don't worry, I give as hard as I take."

"Well, I hope so because this is getting out of control."

My iPhone went off a second time.

"Can you not answer that long enough to pay me some attention?"

"I have to keep up with things Ferrell or they will spin out of control." I looked at my screen and laid the phone down.

Ferrell jumped up from the sofa, "Go ahead and answer the fuckin' phone!"

I jumped up and rushed to grab her and wrapped my arms around her, "I apologize," then kissed her lips.

She kissed me back and we began missing each other in different places until I snatched Ferrell up in my arms and walked back to my bedroom and laid her on the bed, we both started ripping each other's clothes off.

"Make love to me Lion," she said. "Fill me with your passion."

By the time we both were skin naked, I was bulging solid and stood over Ferrell's upstanding breast and leaned forward and sucked her erect nipple in my mouth as I licked the center of her breast down to her navel to her pubic mound that was waxed clean without even a trace of peach fuzz. My lips enveloped her inner lips inside my mouth. Ferrell moaned and reached down with her fingers and spread her lip apart for me to stick my tongue into her core, flicking my tongue in a circular motion and back up to her erectile organ clitoris. Ferrell began to claw at the sheet's the more I sucked on her clitoris and began finger fucking her at the same time.

"It feels so good," she released.

I bit her inner thigh and came back to her lips with small nibbles that caused her to spread her legs apart further and wider. "Oh Lion," she moaned as I stuck a finger inside of her and curled them to come out from the back of her clitoris as I sucked on it from the outside and rocked on her clit back and forth until her juices glisten my finger wet, until she let out a call "Oh god yes!" and "more!" I climbed on top of Ferrell and rocked the head of my penis inside her pink core inch by inch giving her more as I rolled onto my back with her on top.

"Oh Lion!" Ferrell's breast began bouncing out of control as she took every inch of me inside of her walls. Leaning back to grab my ankles, she bent my rod back and rode it, throwing her head up towards the ceiling and rolled around on my dick from her bent knees. Coming forward, Ferrell rolled her hips on top of me getting wetter and wetter. "I want to know what you taste like with me on you," she said, then climbed off of me and turned her ass in my face and started sucking my dick. I spread her ass and sucked her pussy in a sixty/nine, until I was ready to release inside of her. "I'm about to come," I said pulling her off sucking my penis, and tossed her back to the bed, spread her legs into an almost split and rammed my way inside of her wet, hot, juicy kitty until I bust a nut so long and hard my legs trembled.

Halfway through the night, we got to know every part of each other's erections. If I wasn't licking, sticking, and suckling, Ferrell was sucking, and being fucked from wet to dry to wet again.

Finally, after every corner of the sheets had our body fluids on them, we laid in our passion with crust, sweat, and creme from our head to our toes. We took a shower, changed the sheets and climbed underneath the sheets and tied ourselves into a pretzel of sex combinations refusing to allow our bodies to be disconnected.

By putting off having sex with Ferrell, it only built up the sexual tension, and became the release for our lust and desire to reconnect on a physical level.

"That was worth the wait," Ferrell said between the sheets.

"I'll second that."

Ferrell interlocked her fingers between mine and for the first time, both rings had joined as one body.

"You better take that," Ferrell said with the glow of sex in her smile, nodding towards my phone.

"I thought no phones were allowed."

She giggled, "Too much work and no play isn't good for you."

"Does that mean you're in charge of the fore and after play?"

"If you'll be the boss of mine, I'll the first lady boss of yours."

"Think the world can handle that?"

"If not, it better get ready."

"I'll be back, First Lady." I kissed Ferrell shoulder as she laid on her stomach falling asleep, rolled over to the side of the bed, grabbed my phone, and headed to the bathroom looking at the caller's number who had been blowing my phone up.

⟨✼✼✼⟩

"Yeah," I answered the phone, closing the bathroom door behind me.

Turned on the shower and adjusted the temperature of the water, grabbed a rag and bar of Zest soap.

"This is a collect call from," (a recording said): "Je'Niece Blanton. To accept press, zero. If you wish to deny the call press —"

I pressed zero to avoid the full recording. It was the worst time for Je'Niece to be calling me from jail.

"Hello," Je'Niece said.

"Come on bitch, you time is up!" a background voice yelled.

"He just picked up," Je'Niece appealed to the hostile voice.

"Hello," another voice answered the phone.

"I told you nobody answered the first time!" Je'Niece yelled back.

"Who is this?" I asked.

"This is Officer Doris Rhinehart of the 12th Precinct. We're holding Je'Niece Blanton for fleeing the scene of a hit and run accident."

"Okay," I said, "and can I ask why you are intercepting her call?"

"Ms. Blanton has exceeded her call time by making several calls."

"Well, Miss. Blanton just cleared the line when you took the phone from her. I can't speak for any other calls but if you put her back on the phone, I'm sure she'll pass the phone."

"Make it quick," officer Doris said to Je'Niece.

"Hello Lion, you have to come get me out of here. They're charging me with hit and run some old bum."

"You hit somebody with my car?"

"Kinda."

"Je'Niece how do you kinda hit someone? Either you did or you didn't."

"Lion, can I explain it to you late? Just come get me."

"Can't your mother come get you?"

"She won't answer her phone and they impounded your car."

"I'm on my way, Je'Niece."

"Thank you, thank you, thank you!" Je'Niece sounded relieved. "And Lion, I think I'm going to need a lawyer."

"Did you give a statement to the police?"

"No, but they keep asking me questions about you." "About me, what kind of questions?"

"I don't know, stupid stuff like was I with you last night and how long have I had your car, stuff like that."

"Anything else?"

"I got to pee, and I'm not using this nasty toilet, so could you please hurry up and come get me before I have to pee on myself."

"I'm on my way and don't tell the cops shit about me, do you understand?"

"I understand."

I jumped in the water and did a 360-turn wash down and was out before the soap was completely off of my body, got dressed and was out the door while Ferrell had been put to sleep.

Chapter 41

12TH PRECINCT HAD ITS REPUTATION FOR VIOLATING human and civil rights of its suspended detainees.

"Hi," I said, approaching the clericals desk, "I'm Mr.—"

""Lion," the desk officer completed. "We've been waiting to talk to you, Mr. Lion!" he said in a loud voice.

It was right then that I knew it was not going to be a good day and Je'Niece had not told me everything she had told the police about me. The loudmouth clerk raised his voice to draw the attention he sought and in no time at all, I was being approached by whom I knew to be vice officers.

"Mr. Lion Dupri Marsalis?"

"Marsalis," I corrected his mispronunciation.

"I'm sorry, Marsalis. Is that you?"

"Yes, it is."

His partner beamed a smile. "Mr. Lion," he gleefully said, "did you bring your lawyer with you?

"Do I need to call him?"

"If you own a black Jaguar and know a young lady by the name of —""Let's cut through the bullshit and tell me what's this all about."

The fake professional smile left the vice officer's face.

"How about you're under arrest you smart motherfucker! Now turn your Black ass around and put your hands behind your back."

"For what?" I questioned.

"Murder you son of a bitch, and don't make me tell you again to turn around. PUT YOUR HANDS ON THE DESK AND SPREAD YOUR LEGS!"

He was going for his weapon at the same time his words escalated, and just as I was about to comply, I saw Je'Niece coming from the back of the holding tank, with no cuffs on.

"They made me do it, Lion!" She tried to head towards me but was cut off by an officer.

"Made you do what, Je'Niece?!" I tried to turn to face her.

Just that fast, everything spun out of control. I was rough handled, to say the least and did a little resisting in defense of my safety. A few blows were exchanged, knees thrown with me coming out on the losing end, and quickly landing on my shoulder in a filthy dry cell. The back wall was the only thing that kept my face from entering the adjacent cell.

"Hope you got a taste of that sweet ass because it's gonna be the last taste of freedom you'll get," one cop said, straightening his uniform from the scuffle.

If I was not so preoccupied with trying to get myself up off the floor, I'm sure I would have had a slick retort for the flatfooted beat walking cop. But I did manage to get a good long-lasting look at his face. I sat down and immediately realized I had made a major blunder by not telling Ferrell I was leaving the house, where I was going, nor did I call Castro to let him know that I was walking freely into a police precinct

.About twenty minutes later, "Mr. Lion!" another cop calls me out.

I did not respond, just sat there looking at him like the trapped lion in a cage that I was.

"We'd like to ask you a few questions about um…" he paused to look at his clipboard. "Yeah, a Medina Duncan."

"Sorry but I don't know anybody by that name," I flat out lied.

"But you do know Je'Niece Blanton?"

"Do I?"

"She was under the wheel of your vehicle and says you have a girlfriend named Medina that the two of you went Christmas shopping for."

"Why don't you ask my lawyer if I know either one of them."

The homicide cop chuckled. "Always the first thing a guilty person says."

"Lots of innocent people found that out the hard way," I said. "And maybe your Je'Niece asked for her attorney before you started questioning her and wasn't complied with."

That removed the stupid smirk from the cop's face.

"Have it your way, Mr. Lion," he said. "But I assure you if we find just one of your grimy prints at Duncan's house, you'll never see the light of day from the other side of these bars." Those were his last words as he scribbled on his pad and left.

"Son of a bitch," I mumbled.

"Damn killer!" a caged voice came from the cell across from me.

I just looked at him, not liking the title he'd hung on me.

"You wouldn't happen to have a smoke, would you?"

"I don't smoke," I responded.

"Sounds like they got you by the balls, baby."

"You a lawyer or a jailhouse snitch?"

He laughed. "Naw, homie but it don't take a genius to know when the gig is up, and the way you did the electric slide across that floor, I'd say that was your great exit off the world stage to the big house."

If penitentiary was full of jailhouse lawyers doling out advice like this guy, then no wonder the prisons were so packed.

"Hey homie," the mouth that never stopped talking called out to me.

"What?"

"That yo' all black Jag in the lot out there?"

"If it's all black everything, it's mine."

"They putting it on a flatbed towing truck and high-fiving each other."

"Oh yeah."

I had heard it all before, but I would have never believed it could have happened to me. Of all the things I could have been sent to prison for that I was guilty of, that I had gotten away with, the one thing I was not guilty of was about to sink me. There was not a doubt in my mind that my fingerprints were all over Medina's house. Hell, I practically lived there, had touched every dish, sat on every piece of furniture in that house and worst of all, I had clothes still hanging in her closet.

I guess my cellmate jailhouse attorney was right — it didn't take a genius to know that the boys in the big house was stamping out my prison numbers before a jury of my peers came back with a guilty verdict on all counts.

Chapter
42

TWO PEOPLE CAN KEEP A SECRET WHEN ONE OF THEM IS DEAD.

My first visitor in the Wayne County Jail was Castro. I was escorted to a booth the size of a southern outhouse; the only difference was this one had a three-inch plate glass as a divider between myself the visitor. I had to sit there until he was brought up to six southwest, the floor where they kept those who were being held for murder and could not post bail, and were retained to the county because the judge believed they posed a flight risk, or inmates who were back on appeals from the state's penitentiary.

Wayne County prosecutors won the battle over trying me on first degree murder because they issued a warrant to expedite me, saying Medina's murder was committed in their jurisdiction and the body was later moved to West Bloomfield to cover up the crime scene. It was a power move on both sides. My attorneys felt we stood a better chance of getting the charges dropped from first degree to second degree or manslaughter if we managed to get the case before one of our judges, which turned out not to be the case because the Wayne County prosecutor immediately went judge shopping to find a judge who would do their bidding. After five judges refused to take my case, the prosecution managed to find the most conservative judge on the bench.

As if things couldn't get any worse, the former mayor of the city had just received a commutation from the outgoing president, which had the city divided. After being consumed by my own thoughts for twenty minutes, Castro strolled in. His demeanor spoke volumes and he could hardly look me in the eyes, sat down, and dropped his head, shaking it from side to side.

I sat there looking at him and if I wasn't the one sitting in the hot seat, I would have thought he was the one facing charges.

"I got bad news," Castro finally spoke, looking at me through the hand stained glass.

"Stacking a cherry on top of a pile of shit don't make it sweet, so just give it to me raw," I said.

"I was at the interrogation house last night tying up some loose ends on Pharaoh and was scared shitless when I got down to the basement and found Holiday sitting down there with third and fourth degree burns from head to toe." Castro dropped his head and took a deep breath before continuing, "His flesh was hanging from his face and the skin that was his eyelids has been totally burnt off. It almost killed me to see him like that and he's just in bad shape all the way around." He looked up at me. "Got any ideas how he got that way?"

"He didn't say?"

"He was not in much of a mood for talking," Castro choked down his words.

"What's he taking for the pain?"

"No matter what he's taking man, he can't survive this without medical attention."

"He wouldn't be in the basement if he felt that was an option for him, Castro."

He just sat there waiting for me to give him the order. "Clean this up without delay."

"Just like that?"

"This is the business we're in, and hard decisions must be made."

"You know the longer I'm in this business, the more I'm starting to question what we're doing. Seems like we're causing more harm than doing good."

"You and I both know when you start second guessing yourself, it's either time to get out or you start to make slips in judgment."

"But I'm not you, Lion."

"You don't have to be me to keep things in order."

"I'm not talking about that."

"Then what are you talking about?"

"We've known Holiday before this shit hit the streets and now you're asking me to —"

"Look, Castro," I leaned in closer to the glass, "this ain't no confession booth where you get to do seven Hail Mary's to clear your conscience. Holiday is Holiday, and if he's in as bad shape as you say he is, I don't know why this is even a discussion and you didn't make this decision before you came up here."

"You're right, you're right. I'll clean this up as soon as I leave here."

"My man," I said and sat back in my chair.

Holiday was in no mood to talk, and I had to be reassured that his silence stayed permanent. He was the only one who could link me to Mr. Valentino's untimely demise, and two people can keep a secret when one of them is dead.

Castro looked at me and nodded his head up and down. "So, what's the lawyers saying?" he asked. "We paid them, and I called to find out what's with all the postponements and they telling me some shit about attorney-client privilege and I have to ask you."

"They working on a cop."

"A cop, you gonna cop a plea?" he asked. "For how long, and you think the family can take that kind of hit?"

"I don't know how long. Until the offer is put in writing and the family isn't taking this hit, I am."

"You know what I mean man. This shit started falling apart the moment word got out that you're locked up facing a life sentence. You got family members climbing over each other and other families calling meetings down at the Brotherhood to vote you out as chairman. I can't hold this shit together because I didn't put it together."

"You have another visitor, Mr. Lion." A Wayne County deputy opened the door and said, "She's on her way up."

I looked over my shoulder. "Thank you," and turned my attention back to Castro.

"What about you?" he said.

"What about me?"

"Mr. Lion," he pointed out. "Word is you've already made a name for yourself in here."

"In here, they don't give a fuck about who you were out there, so Don don't mean shit unless you're prepared to defend it."

"But that's not your world."

"It is until I'm free."

"Just don't bury yourself in there by making things worse than they already are, is all I'm saying." He put his fist to the glass, and I met it with my fist just as the door behind him came open. "Call me later and I'll let you know how the clean-up went."

"Will do," I said while looking over his shoulder as he stood up to leave.

"Hey, Castro."

"How you doing, Joyce?" they said in passing each other.

Joyce sat down, but unlike Castro she looked me square in the eyes.

"Hi," she said after taking off her coat and having a seat.

"So what brings you down here?" I asked to get straight to the point.

She just sat there looking at me without saying a word.

"Okay, since you didn't answer my first question, let's try this. Who sent you down here?"

"The family is concerned about you, Lion."

"In what regard?"

"Well, just because you chose to be too busy to check up on anyone doesn't mean no one cares about you."

"You gonna get to the point or do this one-two step to get to why you're here?"

"You know why I'm here, Lion."

"Then all you need to do is tell me who gave Pharaoh those drugs down at that hospital."

"Why, what difference would it make?"

I felt my blood beginning to boil with each word that came out of Joyce's mouth. She was the one person in the family everyone went to in order to avoid coming directly to me with their grievances.

"So that means you know who did it?"

"No," she shook her head from side to side. "When does it stop?"

"When does what stop, Joyce?"

"The killing!?" She raised her voice. "If I tell you, you're just going to have them killed and the killing has to stop at some point."

"So that's what you come down here to tell me or you just had to see me locked up with your own eyes?"

"I did not come down here to fight with you."

"But you came here knowing I was going to ask you about Pharaoh."

"I'm not going to do this with you, and do you think this is what Pharaoh would want you to do?"

"Don't think you can come down here and lecture me about what Pharaoh wanted."

"Well, somebody needed to. You're sitting here on your way to prison for murdering your girlfriend and plotting who knows how many other deaths. If you just need to kill someone, then why don't you just kill me because I'm not telling you anything that's going to get someone killed."

"Then you wasted your time coming down here."

"So does that mean I'm next?"

"If you jump in front of a moving bullet, do you think it's going to go around you or through you?"

"Okay," Joyce said with a nervous grin on her face. "I didn't mean all of that, Lion. I mean I know what you're capable of doing and I'm not trying to provoke you."

"You come down here and accuse me of murdering Medina and you don't think you're provoking me?" I asked, fuming with anger. "On advice of my overpaid attorneys, they're recommending I go in a courtroom and plead guilty for a crime I did not commit in order to keep from being sent away for the rest of my life. And you're talking to me like you know what happened in my relationship? I think we're done here!"

"Why must you have everyone fear you like you're crazy or something?" Joyce said, getting up and putting her coat back on. "Are you going to say goodbye to me?" she asked. "Just don't shoot the messenger, okay?" were her final words as she looked back at me before leaving out the door.

I sat there until the Deputy came to escort me back to my cell. It was always awkward having law officials paying their respects via their affiliates as a way for the badge. It wasn't until then that I realized how much clout the Legion family had outside the underworld and made their way into the legal enterprises. It's not what you know but who you know that makes the world go round.

Chapter 43

MONEY CAN'T BUY LOVE, BUT IT CAN TILT THE SCALES of justice.

My attorneys convinced me to take the plea deal negotiated with the prosecutor, and although the judge was a conservative asshole, he was reasonable. It was hard to tell after receiving twenty-five to life on a reduced charge of second-degree murder, but they contended it was only a PR appeasement and they'd get a resentencing once the case died down and somebody else got the Most Wanted spotlight.

The case against me had very little to do with Medina Duncan. It was about a street thug turned Don of the City, and a message to all those would-be hoodlums that you're not untouchable in the eyes of the law. The State's exhibits consisted of evidence that showed I was a drug warlord who had a way of making people disappear even if my finger wasn't on the trigger, arguing without a shred of evidence that Medina wanted out of the relationship and because she knew too much, I gave her no other way out than to kill her.

As it turned out, Je'Niece was not only never a potential prosecution witness, but the hit and run never came up in any of the proceedings. My attorneys had no idea what I was talking about when I told them how I ended up being down at the police precinct. There was no record of Je'Niece ever being arrested. She disappeared and the cops alleged that I had walked into the station exhibiting signs of being high off PCP.

Ferrell had turned into a lush for six months and attributed her drinking for her morning sicknesses until the bulge in her stomach started kicking. It was only after having little Andrew Lion Valentino that Ferrell began to refocus her desire to accept the cards she was dealt.

Castro held things down as best he could until being a family man became a higher priority. The Lion family became a splinter group spending more time battling over territory than they made money, drawing the attention of the Feds until they were picked up one by one. Still, no one knew how a man suffering third and fourth-degree burns managed to make it all the way from Florida back to Michigan without blinking an eye. All I know is, two people can keep secret when one is dead.

With Holiday making it back from Florida, I was no longer concerned about my meeting with Don Mondavi. Which meant I was still the Don of the Legion-Lion family, or what was left of them anyway. My rings? They were personally picked up by Ferrell along with my other personal belongings. If I did have to serve my full prison term, Li'L Lion would have to take up where

I left off, starting with settling all old family business. I mean, after all, it was a family business, and we are what we inherit.

Then there were the Tokyo Twins, who for the life of me, I could not explain how women who could be arch-enemies one moment and BFFs once a baby is thrown into the equation. That is to say, after Li'l Lion was born, the twins and Ferrell had discovered a common interest that made them inseparable as business partners after Ferrell had crowned the twins Andrew Lion Valentino's godmothers.

David had not surfaced, who somehow managed to escape the explosion of the yacht that killed Andrew. The old man was merely collateral damage. There's nothing like solitary confinement to make a man think, all of which came crashing down on me as I stood in my nine-by-eighteen looking out the rear window trying to organize my thought's until I heard a soft thump, looked over my shoulder and with no one in sight, an iPhone-12 had been tossed on my bed. Just as I picked it up, a gallery porter pushing a dust broom had doubled back to make sure I had received the package, saying it was from the family. I smiled, realizing at that moment my power didn't end by being behind bars.

A few minutes later, a corrections officer came pass and I cuffed the iPhone. She asked what I was concealing behind my back, and I just stood there for a minute thinking I had just been set up. But she smiled and said her shift was about to end and to let her know if I needed anything else before she went home.

As for the person who shot drugs into Pharaoh's intravenous bag, they say keep your enemies close and your family closer because those who can hurt you deepest aren't your enemies outside, but those on the inside closest to you. Those we least expect to bring us harm will be the ones capable of getting close enough to stick the knife in your back. I had eliminated all outside possibilities to discover multiple insurance policies had been taken out on Pharaoh by his wife and in-laws — not old but recent policies leading up to his overdose. Whether friend, family, or foe that took out a policy on Pharaoh's untimely demise was unfinished family business.

I tied a sheet to one corner of the bars and did the same to the opposite bars to create a curtain for privacy. Went to the back of the cell, sat on the toilet, and dialed the General's number of the Crazy Eight's. He picked up after a couple rings as if expecting my call. "I'm texting you an address," I said. "Make them feel my reach." That was the end of my power on the streets and the beginning of the Don of the City from behind bars.

The end is really the beginning.

About the Author

MICHAEL C. PARKER IS ALSO THE AUTHOR OF SPOOKY. His works include *Crossing the Line Marked in Blood, Dead Ain't Enough, and Nightshade.* He is also the designer and patent & trademark owner of the Spooky Apparel @spookytheunderdog. com, and co-designer of Platinum Eyecandy as well as the Divine Diva DK brand.

Printed in the United States
by Baker & Taylor Publisher Services